The Girl in the Wall

Daphne Benedis-Grab

MeritPress

F+W Media, Inc.

For my mom

Published by Merit Press
an imprint of F+W Media, Inc.
10151 Carver Road, Suite 200
Blue Ash, Ohio 45242. U.S.A.
www.meritpressbooks.com

Trade Paperback ISBN 10: 1-4405-8282-3
Trade Paperback ISBN 13: 978-1-4405-8282-0
Hardcover ISBN 10: 1-4405-5270-3
Hardcover ISBN 13: 978-1-4405-5270-0
eISBN 10: 1-4405-5271-1
eISBN 13: 978-1-4405-5271-7

Printed in the United States of America.

10 9 8 7 6 5 4 3 2 1

Cover design by Frank Rivera.
Cover image © iStockphoto.com/Coffee&Milk/Jasmina007.

This book is available at quantity discounts for bulk purchases.
For information, please call 1-800-289-0963.

Acknowledgments

I am extremely lucky to be represented by Sara Crowe, the best cheerleader and sharpest businesswoman a writer could hope to have in her corner. Huge thanks to my editor Jacquelyn Mitchard, who has been wonderful and wise throughout. Donna Freitas, Marie Rutkoski, Rebecca Stead, Lisa Graff, and Eliot Schrefer are my dream team of readers and I owe them many thanks, as well as a plate of scones. Thanks to my family and friends who supported me through all kinds of neurotic meltdowns, with a special shout out to my husband Greg. And last but not least, my kids Ainyr and Erlan, who made it clear they'd tolerate me writing a book so long as I put their names somewhere in it.

CHAPTER 1

Sera

What do you wear to the birthday party of your ex-best friend? The one who dumped you flat in the middle of junior year, turning the entire student body against you in the process, and who has made your life hell for the nine months and four days since?

I debate calling my dad and asking yet again if I really have to go to Ariel's seventeenth party, the first one we didn't plan together since she turned eight. But that would be a waste of time, I know what he'll say. He'll talk about his friendship with Simon Barett, my dad being the only person in the world who calls Mr. Barett by his first name, about how they were best friends in college, about how my dad's investments in Barett Pharmaceuticals helped make it the thriving, billion-dollar business it is today. About how friendships have ups and downs but some things, like the Barett and French family bond, are forever. Which means that regardless of a "small tiff" (his words), I need to be there for Ariel's big day.

With a slight crackle the intercom in my room comes to life. "Honey, the car will be ready to take you in ten minutes," my mom says.

Yes, our house is big, like all the houses in our town of New Canaan, Connecticut. But my mom could walk the distance from her bedroom down the hall to tell me this. She, however, is avoiding me. The thought of going to this party has made me "difficult" (her word) and she'd rather not deal with me face to face. In fairness I have picked an awful lot of fights with her in the past nine months and four days.

Ten minutes to select the outfit that will be ridiculed all night by the senior class of New Canaan Country Day School, along with my hairstyle, shoes, and the way I breathe. The school is small with an elite group of hand-selected students, each of whom treats me like a total pariah.

I lose no matter what choices I make, so I opt for comfortable: jeans that show off my yoga body (lots of time for working out when you have no social life), black cami, and a silky black cashmere sweater. It's October and the nip of fall is in the air. I slide my feet into comfortable black flats, pull my hair up in a loose ponytail with a few wispy curls floating around my face. I grab my little black purse that I've already stuffed with my wallet, house keys, and cell phone, plus the Swiss Army knife my dad insists I carry with me at all times, and my overnight bag. Because, of course, this is no ordinary party, not with Mr. Barett funding it. It's a full weekend of celebration, starting with a private concert with Hudson Winters.

Okay, I have to admit that is the one thing I'm excited about. I love Hudson's music. Not the few pop songs that made him famous but the ones that are more like folk rock with a dash of something almost like bluegrass thrown in. The ones with the lyrics that are so honest they resonate somewhere deep inside each time I listen to them. Which is pretty much daily since I'm not going out a lot these days and I need something to keep me company.

My phone chirps, a sound I used to hear hundreds of times a day. Now it makes me jump. I pick it up and see the text from my sister Samantha.

Good luck 2nite

She remembered. It's like drinking a hot cup of cocoa after being out in the sleet.

Think it may kill me I write back.

Hi-school sucks. Remember in 11 months you will be here

Sam is a sophomore at Brown and she loves it. I still have to get in but it's a pretty sure thing. My grades are stellar, my extracurriculars pitch perfect, and the huge donations my alumni dad gives every year don't hurt.

Love u she writes.

My sister is probably the only reason I've survived these past months.

I type and send a heart icon, and then slip my phone back in my purse.

There's no avoiding it: I'm ready. I go down the huge curving staircase to our foyer that is filled with orchids, my mother's passion. I complain that it smells like a perfume shop every time I open the front door but really I love the rich, gentle scent of the velvety pink, lavender, and white blooms. The car driving me is waiting. I take a last, longing look at my house, then slide onto the buttery leather seat and accept the fate that awaits me.

It's impossible not to be impressed as the car drives through the carefully cultivated woods guarding the Barett estate from the road and you see the mansion for the first time. New Canaan houses are big but none as big and elegant as this. Its cream-colored wings and turrets and towers make it seem more like a plantation from the Old South than the modern-day suburbs of New York City. Ariel and I went through a brief *Gone with the Wind* phase back when we were eleven and it truly felt like we were at Tara.

That was also when we discovered the secret passages that twine through the walls of the house. We had a great time spying from inside the walls until the terrible Saturday night when we peeked through the grate into her father's bedroom. Mr. Barett was in there with Stella, the woman who became his second wife two months later, and it was possibly the night that Abby, Ariel's baby sister, was conceived. That image of the two of them, which is unfortunately seared into my brain forever, still makes me feel like I ate a rotten clam.

The rolling green lawns are broken up by gardens and artfully placed trees. I see a few of the gardeners lurking about, which is unusual on a Saturday evening. I guess Mr. Barett is making sure everything is perfect.

My car rounds the circular drive and stops at the front door, which is flanked by columns.

"We're here, Sera," Evan, the driver, says.

We don't have a regular driver but the car company we use often sends Evan and he's really nice. For a moment I play with the idea of asking him to drive me away, into town, into the city, anywhere, really, that isn't here. But I'm sure he's under strict orders from my dad.

"Thanks," I say. "Have a good night."

He smiles and I step out onto the smooth stone path that leads up to the house. The door opens before I knock but it's not James, the head of household who usually opens the door at the Barett's. Something else that's changed I guess.

The man who opened the door has blond hair and a tight smile, and he seems awkward as he ushers me into the huge foyer of the Barett home. James definitely had better social graces. I wonder what happened to him.

The huge marble staircase sweeps up to the second floor, famous paintings placed along the way. The huge black-and-white marble foyer has two actual trees in it, bonsais with dark, twisted trunks and artfully shaped branches. There is a large white chest where I realize I am to put my overnight bag. I hesitate. What are the chances it will mysteriously disappear if I leave it with the others?

Over the past nine months and four days I have gotten a hard lesson in what it means to be a pariah and I know the chances are high, so the bag stays with me. I smile at the blond guy and keep my backpack on. He starts to say something but the doorbell rings again. He goes to answer it and I slip off toward the west wing of the house. The east wing has the fancy living room, dining room, glassed-in sunroom, and library. Around back, in the newest wing, is Mr. Barett's home office suite.

I go into the west wing, through the living room, my chest tight as I try to ignore the fact that this used to be my second home. It smells exactly the same, like a mix of grapefruit-scented cleaner, fresh roses, and burning wood from the fireplace. One wall is all windows and I take a second to slow my breathing, looking out on the French garden. The sun is low in the sky and the two gardeners out on the lawn are bathed in shadow. A third joins them holding some kind of weird lawn equipment. Or is it a gun? For a moment my insides clench and then the obvious hits me: They aren't gardeners, they're security. Hudson Winters is here and Mr. Barett must have hired top-notch security.

As I get closer to the game room I hear voices, laughter, the sound of glasses clinking, and my stomach suddenly twists tight. I close my eyes for a moment. I can survive this.

Everyone looks toward the door when I walk in and then looks away, in that way you avert your eyes when you see a homeless man peeing on the sidewalk. I hear whispers, the word "backstabber" hissed just loud enough to make it to my ears. But I am invisible, vapor, a reaction that still makes me feel like garbage.

I try to walk normally, not slink in like a beaten dog, but it's hard, especially when my legs are shaky and I don't have quite enough air in my lungs. I avoid looking at anyone, especially the group sitting on the sofa and chairs around the unlit fireplace. That's where the inner circle, Ariel's circle, will be. I don't want to see Mike, state-ranked soccer player who I used to let cheat off my geometry tests; Ravi who kissed me at the eighth-grade dance, my first ever kiss; Cassidy, queen of slicing gossip who I thought was hysterical until I became the source of the gossip.

And then there's Bianca, my replacement as Ariel's best friend, who is flaunting the necklace Ariel gave her a few weeks ago, the one that matches her own solid white-gold heart necklace from Tiffany. You could actually call Bianca Ariel's twin because aside from the matching necklaces, Bianca started dying her hair at Vivian's the exact same shade of buttery blond Ariel was born with, and they go together for weekly bangs maintenance and to pick up the French lavender hair products Vivian imports from France. I sat behind Bianca in English and the first time she came in with her new hair, smelling just like Ariel with her wafting lavender, I had to go to the nurse with a crushing headache and eyes that wouldn't stop tearing.

But of course the person I most want to avoid is Ariel herself. I know how she will glance past me like I am invisible, her features hardening just the tiniest bit. I wonder if her new best friend recognizes her sign for pure hatred.

I stuff my purse in my bag and stow it behind the sofa in the back corner of the room and walk over to the bar that has every non-alcoholic drink under the sun and two bartenders ready to serve it. The alcohol is hidden in another room, I'm guessing the study because people seem to be slipping in and out. I won't be welcome in there but that's okay. I'm better off staying sober and alert. Less chance of getting beer "accidently" poured on me if my reflexes are sharp.

I am given a sparkling seltzer fruit punch that is probably delicious but I can't really tell. My taste buds, like the rest of me, go numb when I am near anyone from school.

I drift off to an unoccupied corner of the room. The game room is massive, with leather sofas and armchairs, a pool table, and a huge TV with every video game console sold. Usually small stuffed stools and tables are scattered around but now they, along with the pool table, have been pushed aside to make room for the concert setup.

I feel a tiny shiver of delight when I see the amplifier, guitar, stool, and single mic, with rows of chairs arranged in front. I can't believe I'm going to see Hudson Winters live like this. In the few interviews he's done he comes off as a snob but it's hard to care when his music is so awesome. A big guy lurks nearby, probably Hudson's private bodyguard or something.

"Sera," a commanding voice calls.

I straighten up as Mr. Barett approaches. In his wake is John Avery, his top assistant and Ariel's godfather. He's more like a father to her than Mr. Barett.

"How's your father?" Mr. Barett asks, giving me a solid shoulder slap that nearly topples me.

"Well, thanks," I say. I've known Mr. Barett forever but he still makes me nervous. "He sends his best."

"Trying to get out of that money he owes me on our last round of golf," he says. He reaches into the inside pocket of his jacket and pulls out his sleek phone, a model that hasn't even been released on the market yet, checks a text, and tucks it back in.

Mr. Avery smiles and leans over to kiss my cheek. He smells like the lemon lozenges he sucks to soothe his smoker's throat. Mr. Avery sometimes read us bedtime stories when I had sleepovers here, and from the sympathy in his eyes, I'm guessing he realizes me not being over here for the past nine months and four days means bad things for me. That and the fact I've been totally ignored by my classmates.

"Is Abby here?" I ask, glancing around for signs of Abby who was five the last time I saw her but would be six now. Mr. Barett and his second wife Stella had a nasty divorce and he rarely gets visits with Abby, but Ariel adores her sister so I'm guessing she'll make a birthday appearance at some point.

"Not until tomorrow morning," Mr. Barett says.

It'll be nice to see Abby, if she even remembers me. We used to include her in our games whenever she was over and it made her so happy. Ariel said Stella neglected Abby and that made Ariel really protective of her, probably since she'd been pretty neglected herself.

"So are you looking forward to the concert?" Mr. Barett asks in a proprietary way.

"Yes," I say. "I once read that Hudson Winters doesn't do private shows so this is really cool."

Mr. Barett smiles. "He does if the price is right," he says. Then he frowns as he glances outside. "Though he does seem to require an extraordinary amount of security. Who'd have thought a singer needed that many guards with machine guns?"

I follow his gaze and see several figures standing in the yard, machine guns resting over their shoulders. At least I assume they're machine guns because that's what Mr. Barett said.

"That's what his people said he needed," Mr. Avery says. He would know because he's usually the one to handle details like that for the Barett family.

"And whatever he needs, he gets," Mr. Barett says dryly. "I should have been a rock star."

It's hard not to laugh at that.

"The concert is about to start," Mr. Barett says, apparently having received some kind of signal from somewhere. "Come up front with Ariel. I know she'll want you next to her."

Yeah, she wants that like she wants to give up a kidney.

"Um, actually my ears are kind of sensitive so I think I'll stay back here," I say.

Mr. Barett is about to insist when we hear a commotion, raised voices, a few shrieks. Hudson Winters has arrived. He's wearing beat-up jeans and a black T-shirt and he's even cuter than he is in his videos, with piercing hazel eyes, messy brown curls, and the perfect planes of his face. He's muscular and wide, like a jock, but he moves with a feline grace that makes him even sexier as he picks up his guitar from the stand and settles on the stool, not really looking at anyone. His bodyguard guy lurks near the front of the stage but he mostly looks bored.

Mr. Barett rushes across the huge room, almost tripping over the edge of the hundred-year-old Oriental carpet to get to the mic.

"It's my great pleasure to present Hunter Winters," he says grandly.

I wince at the mistake. Of course Mr. Barett has no idea who Hudson is; he just asked around for the name of the hottest, most exclusive singer and decided that was who needed to headline this party. Ariel's preferences played no part in the choice, not that I feel sorry for her. She is sitting primly in the center of the first row, Bianca on one side of her and her dad now settling in on her other side. John Avery slips out, probably to the upstairs office suite. This kind of music isn't usually popular with old guys who crunch numbers for a living.

The lights overhead are giving off a soft golden glow but it's mostly dark, with the last bit of daylight coming in through the huge windows that line the west side of the room. The right side has the oversized fireplace, the one that's not yet lit. Paintings hang along that wall, one is even an actual Van Gogh, but right now they are just black squares melting into the scenery. The focus is all on Hudson as he strums his guitar lightly and pauses to tune one of the strings.

By now everyone has a seat and I feel safe sitting. Pariahs need to choose seats with care, something I learned the hard way when I went to the end-of-sophomore-year picnic (my mom acted like she might suffer a spontaneous brain aneurysm if I skipped). That night when we were watching the class movie and people were sneaking off to get beer from a keg AJ Green hid in the woods that morning, I was sitting toward the back when a cup of beer got dumped over my head. Sneaking home with beer-soaked clothes and dripping hair was no easy feat and not something I'd like to repeat.

"Hey, I'm Hunter Winters," Hudson says.

I laugh but no one else does. Hudson glances back at me, as do most of my classmates, and I am mortified that I didn't just nod coolly at the joke. I stare down at my hands, my cheeks hot.

"I'm going to start with—" Hudson continues.

Mr. Barett coughs loudly and Hudson stops.

"Right, yeah, happy birthday Ariel," he says, his voice flat. "Sorry I don't do birthday songs." As he launches into his breakout song, "Wanting You," I notice Ariel and Bianca switching seats, their identical blond hair shimmering in the dim light as they resettle. And then I forget Ariel and her followers, that I'm stuck in this terrible place for the entire weekend, and I just sink into the music.

But just as Hudson begins the chorus, the room goes pitch black, the shades falling silently over the windows as the lights are switched off.

Hudson's voice and guitar trail off into an eerie quiet. A girl giggles and for a moment I think it must be some kind of weird joke. It is dark for about thirty seconds and then I hear a sharp popping sound and the lights flare back on.

I see the body first, a crumpled form by the front of the stage, a growing pool of blood coming from underneath it. It's Hudson's bodyguard. In that moment Hudson leaps off the stool and goes to him.

"Everyone on the floor, now," someone barks.

The room is chaos as people dive off their chairs to lie flat on the floor.

I stretch out on my belly, my heart thumping violently in the compressed space between my chest and the floor. I lift my head the tiniest bit to look around, trying to make sense of this thing that makes no sense. The room is filled with the men I thought were Hudson's security team, the ones wearing cargo pants and T-shirts, the ones who now have stocking caps pulled low over their faces. The ones who are carrying guns.

Two of them stride over to where Mr. Barett and Ariel lie prone and pull them up. They expertly fold Mr. Barett and

Ariel's arms behind their backs with one hand while holding guns to their temples with the other. I can't see their faces, just Ariel's long hair swishing as she is jerked toward the door of the living room.

For a moment everyone else is frozen, but then Ella Kim screams and the person holding Mr. Barett flinches. In that millisecond Mr. Barett shakes free and grabs for the gun. I see his fingers wrap around the barrel just as more shots ring out. I instinctively scrunch down squeezing my eyes shut. I expect to hear more screaming but now silence pulsates like a living thing.

I don't want to see what has happened, but not knowing is even worse so I slowly raise my head. My classmates are where they were, still plastered to the floor. For a moment I think everything is okay, or at least the same, but then I look toward the front of the room.

Two more people are lying on the floor, both at odd angles. Each has blood running from a head wound, so fast and thick it's like a faucet has been turned on. My breath is stuck in my chest and for a moment the lack of oxygen makes me light-headed, like I will faint, but still I can't look away from the bodies on the floor. The bodies that are most surely dead.

The bodies that are Mr. Barett and Ariel.

CHAPTER 2

Ariel

When the room goes black I feel my energy coil. It's been a while since I was in actual physical danger but my body remembers and it is prepared. There is a slight rustle behind me and then the shot, loud, makes me jump and leaves the smoky scent of burnt paper in the air. I am up before my mind processes what it was, heading to the fireplace. My fingers are sure as I reach for the catch that springs open the secret door that leads to the hidden passages that wind through my old house. As the lights flicker on I am inside, grate closed firmly behind me. It's only then that I realize I am panting and my heart is pounding with a sickening heaviness inside my chest.

I lean back against the wall of the tunnel and close my eyes. These tunnels go all over the house, at least the old part. The addition my dad had put on, the one with his office suite, doesn't have any. I'm not sure why they are here—the Underground Railroad maybe?—but I also don't think anyone else knows about them. Which means I'm safe for the moment, while I try to figure out what is happening.

I peek out through one of the openings in the grate and gasp. I see a body on the floor. It's not until Hudson rushes over that I realize it's his bodyguard. Someone must be trying to kidnap Hudson. But when I look around to see who's coming for him, I see it's not Hudson they're after at all. It's my dad and Bianca who are being hustled from the room, guns pressed to their temples. For a moment Bianca throws a wild look behind her and I see pure terror in her eyes. Does she know it's me they want, not her? If so, she needs to say something, now.

That's when the screaming starts and I see my dad pulling free, grabbing for the gun. Then it's in his hands, he actually has the gun, can do something, can fight back.

I don't see who fires the shots but I see them fall, first my dad, then Bianca.

And now two more bodies lie on the floor. My dad's head is steadily pumping out blood. Next to him is Bianca, her blond hair matted with red and little flecks of gray, the heart necklace I gave her wet with blood.

I stumble backwards, retching, bile burning the back of my throat. But burning even hotter is the thought that screams in my head. That is supposed to be me on the floor, bleeding to death next to my father. Bianca switched seats with me at the last minute so she could have the better view of Hudson Winters. The chain of my own heart necklace is suddenly searing into me and I tear it off, ripping the delicate links, and throw it in a far corner where it's hidden in shadow.

I am alive and Bianca is dead. And my father—

There is something wet on my face and I realize it's tears. I am crying, which is weird because I don't actually feel anything, just a cold numbness at my core. But tears are there and my nose is started to get stuffed up. Still, I feel nothing, just the surreal emptiness, like a dark cavern where my insides used to be. And the knowledge that I will not look out again at the bodies.

Another shot rings out and I scramble over to the grate, my heart in my throat. I see my classmates stumbling around, crying, a few sitting clumped together on the floor. It takes a minute to see that no one has been hurt. The shot was fired by another man in Army pants and a black ski mask. He is probably the man who shot my father. I am looking at the guy who just made me an orphan. I should probably be crying or hysterical but all I feel is this emptiness, like wind is blowing through a cavern in my center. That and a profound thankfulness that my sister

Abby isn't here. Her mother is a pathetic caretaker, but right now I couldn't be happier that Abby is with her instead of here, in the room where her dad was just killed.

A shiver runs down my spine because if Abby was here, she would probably have been killed too, and that is unthinkable.

"I said to shut up," the guy says, calmly.

Everybody shuts up. The sight of a gun cradled in the arms of a guy who just shot two people will have that effect. Two other people with stocking caps are efficiently wrapping a tarp around the bodies that used to be Bianca and my father like they are meat in a butcher shop. My stomach lurches and I look away.

"Everyone sit down and keep quiet," the guy standing in front says.

Once again, everyone obeys. I glance over to the spot by the microphone and the wrapped bodies are already gone. The rug has been pulled forward to cover any lingering stains. It's as if nothing happened. What's really weird is that now it almost feels like nothing happened, even though rationally I know my entire life has just changed completely. Does this not-feeling mean I am in shock?

It's only then that I think about John Avery. I've known John since I was born. John is the same age as my dad, fifty-five, but he's slight and frail from having bad asthma and looks about ten years older, with his wispy salt-and-pepper hair and deep wrinkles from spending way too much time working. He was the one who came to my kindergarten graduation when my dad had a last-minute business trip to Bermuda. He's the one who brought me roses when I had the lead in the middle school musical and yet again my dad was away. And he's the one who made sure I had follow-up medical attention after the stuff happened in

Mexico. I'm not deluded enough to think he did it out of the kindness of his heart—he did it because his job is to do what my dad says and my dad told him to go film the graduation and the musical and to make sure the Mexico thing was handled. But I think the roses were John's idea. And he really did look proud when I walked across the stage when I was five.

I scan the room but then I remember he left before the concert, not toward the front door but toward the back stairs that lead to the upstairs office suite. He is up there now, probably working on something for my dad, with no idea what is going on down here. Unless they've already killed him too.

And now I finally feel something. First comes fear, with a sharp, metallic taste in my mouth. Then briefly a piercing, biting pain slices down so deep it takes my breath away. Then comes the anger. That one is familiar, my default setting. That one I can handle. It burns icy cold in my belly but we're old friends and I welcome the anger. Anger makes me act and I like action. It's sitting around feeling things like fear and pain that I can't handle.

So I lean back toward the grate, ready to hear what the guy who assassinated my dad has to say for himself.

"This is a hostage situation," he says. "Be aware that the house and grounds are heavily guarded. There is no escape. But no one will hurt you and soon you will be free, as long as you do what we say, when we say it." He pauses, as though to let this sink in. Like anyone is going to go against their orders. They've taken pampered high school students hostage, not Navy SEALS.

"You are free to be in this room, and with permission, the bathroom, and the kitchen. Anyone who steps outside of these rooms will be shot." One of the girls gasps. It is surprising to hear him say those words in the same exact tone he used to assure everyone that no one would get hurt. "Right now we need your cell phones, cameras, and computers. The agent in back will collect those."

The agent in back has a big bag and he or she begins walking around the room. I look back at the first gunman, the one who murdered my dad and Bianca. Years ago Sera and I watched a movie on late-night cable about a guy who terrorized a small town, shooting defenseless people point blank on the street, and they called him The Assassin. That's who this guy is.

It's probably weird that I'm sitting around thinking about an old movie when my dad is dead (not thinking about that) and my party is being held hostage. But then according to the psychiatrist my dad made me see after the Mexico stuff, I have issues with handling "vulnerable" feelings.

The Assassin watches closely as the agent in back goes around, but everyone is eager to do exactly what they are told and soon the agent in back is filling a bag with the newest, most expensive technology money can buy.

As the collection continues I think about what The Assassin said. It's a good plan. The party is supposed to last all weekend so by the time any parents would expect their kids home or call to check up on them, The Assassin, his boss, and his agents will be long gone. I wonder how they knew about the party—the details were under wraps for security reasons. I'm guessing they paid off one of the household staff to find out the exact plan. My dad isn't exactly the nicest boss so it probably wouldn't have even taken that much. And if they somehow came in under the guise of being security for Hudson Winters, then it was really the perfect opportunity. They sweep in, take their hostages and—

Wait. Their hostage was supposed to be me. Wasn't it? I know Hudson Winters is probably a millionaire, as are a bunch of kids in my class, but that's loose change to my dad, whose company brings in billions every quarter. We are beyond rich so if they're coming in here with machine guns, we are the obvious ones to take. Which is why we were being led from the room at gunpoint. Well, my dad and the person they thought was me. So what happens now, when their hostage is gone and the source of their money is dead? How could they have killed the person who was going to give them what they wanted?

The answer I come up with has me suddenly shivering in a cold sweat. There is one last party guest still to arrive tonight, one who wasn't planning to show up until after the concert because he said "teenager music" gives him a headache. My dad told him that was a surprise considering he lived his life like an eternal teenager but he just laughed, like he always does. That's my Uncle Marc. Immature, yes, but seriously the nicest guy. And the only person besides my dad who can touch the company funds. I don't even want to know what they'd do to get him to sign over the money but Marc is pretty wimpy. I don't see him holding out very long if they start pulling out his fingernails or whatever it is guys like this do to get what they want.

I have to do something to warn him. He was supposed to get here around eight but knowing Marc that means nine. That gives me—I check my watch—two hours. I stand up, ready to start making a plan, but then I hear The Assassin's voice again. He is holding the bag stuffed with phones.

"Just in case anyone thought it might be a clever idea to hold back a phone or computer device, we have cut off all Internet service to the house," The Assassin announces. "And anyone caught with a cell phone will be shot, though first we will shoot the two people nearest to you, just so you understand our feelings about your lack of respect for our orders."

Wow, these guys are so not here to play. But then why would they be? What's at stake is a multibillion-dollar fortune.

"Every room is guarded including the bathroom so the only thing you will not have is privacy. But eat, talk quietly, and sleep, whatever you want. In twenty-four hours it will be over and you will be safe and sound back in your mansions." He gives a small salute and heads out, leaving the other agents to watch over the group.

I stagger back against the wall. Twenty-four hours. He said we'd be kept hostage for twenty-four hours. Earlier, when he said "soon" I assumed they'd be finished and out of here by midnight. But twenty-four hours means they will still be here tomorrow at noon. That's when Stella is dropping off Abby so she can help me celebrate my birthday.

I close my eyes as I think of Abby, with her timid brown eyes, fuzzy brown curls, and the rabbit I gave her when she turned three, Mr. Ears. She takes Mr. Ears with her everywhere, even though he's stained and smells bad and Stella keeps trying to bribe her to take up with a sleeker toy. I think of the last time I saw her, two weeks ago, her eyes full of tears when she told me her mom was going away to a California spa less than two days after getting back from a three-week shopping spree in Paris. I took her up to my room and we had a tea party with Mr. Ears, complete with make-believe fairy cake and sparkle tea. It doesn't take much to make Abby beam like the world is the greatest place ever and it kills me that her mom can't do it more. But not the way it kills me to think of her being dropped off in the middle of this to take my place as a hostage.

My stomach burns as I think about what I can do to stop this. There has to be *something*. I start walking, hoping that will help me think. The tunnels are dim but there are enough grates along the way that it's never actually dark inside them, not unless all the lights in the house are off. With their chipping plaster walls the tunnels are about as wide as a doorway so they're easy to navigate. The ceiling is low but high enough that someone a few inches taller than my five feet five inches could still stand upright. It goes without saying they are also dusty and full of cobwebs and mice droppings. My feet kick up small dust clouds as I go.

My dad is such a neat freak he'd flip if he knew any part of his house looked like this. The thought comes from out of nowhere and hits me like a baseball bat. My dad *was* a neat freak. I can't breathe. I put my head down and try to pull air into my lungs. This is not my first panic attack but they don't really get easier. And there's this thing in my belly, this wail or primal grief that I have to tamp down or it might destroy me. I breathe furiously, focusing my mind on this moment, on the need to put one foot in front of the other and start doing something. I can't fall apart, not when Abby is going to be dropped off in the middle of this. I have to keep it together for her. After a few moments my breathing slows and I can move again.

I walk straight back until I hit the stairs, then I go up and turn left. My bedroom is the third grate down. Some of the grates are in the hall and they look like grates for the heating system, wrought iron with carved flowers and leaves. But mine is like the one I climbed into—it's the back of a fireplace. All of them have small metal latches so they can be easily opened and closed.

My room is dark, with light spilling in through the half-open door. I open the grate as quietly as I can and step silently into the fireplace. Then I walk into the room and that's when I realize I am not alone. Someone else is in here, someone dressed in cargo pants and a white T-shirt, and he turns when he hears me.

CHAPTER 3

Sera

My insides are churning and my skin feels funny, like it doesn't fit right. My mind is like a scratched DVD, playing one image, then suddenly skipping, out of order, to another. Mr. Barett bleeding on the floor. Bianca, her head a soggy mess of red and gray. The guys who look like soldiers guarding the doorways of the house I practically grew up in. And that awful man who reminds me of The Assassin from that old movie calmly telling us that we'll get shot if we step out of the west wing. How did this night go from birthday party to hostage situation? It's too much to take in, to understand, so my mind just keeps skipping back and forth from image to image.

I hated Bianca so much these past nine months but her being killed is so much bigger than that. I can't even think about her mom who always cheered wildly at her soccer games and her younger brother who had a shirt made with Bianca's number on it. This is going to destroy them.

I know my classmates are thinking the same thing and probably talking about it as they sit on the sofas in the corner, huddled together. Or talking about the fact that the agents thought they had Ariel but ended up killing Bianca and that Ariel is now gone. I was probably the last person to realize that but no one told the agents, not that The Assassin was taking questions or comments. I'm guessing that everyone is speculating on where Ariel went but I bet I'm the only one with the right answer. She's got to be in the tunnels. The grounds are covered, the rest of the house is covered, and I doubt the agents know about the tunnels.

No one is asking me what I think, even though we all know I was Ariel's best friend a lot longer than Bianca was. It's kind of unbelievable but even now, in a hostage situation where our lives hang in the balance, no one from NCCD will speak to me. Social status trumps everything I guess. I hope they don't poll the room to see which hostage is voted most expendable.

It's awful in this room where there's a lingering scent of burnt paper and the off-center rug hiding blood and I don't want to know what else—I can't believe we have to stay in here for twenty-four hours. My classmates have all moved off to the group of sofas and chairs closest to the study. Hudson is still on his stool, staring moodily at his hands. I wonder if he knew his bodyguard well. But it's not like I'm going to go talk to him or anything.

Sitting here by myself in the center of this empty group of folding chairs is making me feel exposed. I glance around at the other seating options. There's the poker table with five chairs around it by the front wall or the small sofa and loveseat by the other end of the room, next to one of those floor-to-ceiling windows. I decide on the sofa and am about to stand up when something on the floor catches my eye.

It's tucked under the edge of the rug and if the light weren't glinting off the small corner sticking out, I'd never have noticed it. I'm not positive what it is so I move closer, trying to look casual, then bend down like I need to adjust my shoe. Which is a ballet flat that doesn't need adjustment, but hopefully no one will notice.

Now that I'm down next to it I see that it's a cell phone. My body is suddenly electrified with adrenaline because it's not just anyone's cell phone: It's the phone Mr. Barett took out of his jacket less than an hour ago to check his text. It must have slid out of his pocket when he fell. It's so small and thin you'd barely notice it even if you were sitting right next to it.

Obviously the thing to do is tell one of the agents. It'll win me points with them and since we're all here in this heavily guarded room it's not like I can use the phone to make a call or anything. And following directions, being a good girl, is what I always do.

So the fact that I rest my hand on the phone, clutch it in my palm, and slide it into the sleeve of my sweater, then get up and walk to the sofa on the far back wall, has me feeling like I've stepped into another dimension. A dimension where I'm brave and do things rather than just react.

I last in the new dimension for about ten seconds, feeling brave and excited about myself. Then the panic sets in. What have I done? What the hell am I going to do with this? And what will happen to me if they found out I took it? This isn't a movie where the bad guys are going to make bumbling errors that allow me to be some kind of hero. These are seasoned pros and I'm a pampered suburban girl whose harshest life experience has been getting the silent treatment from my former friends. I can't believe I've done something this stupid.

I have to get rid of it but I'm not sure how. Maybe I can go to the bathroom and just leave it there. But then when someone finds it they'll know it was placed there and you know they'll keep track of who went into the bathroom when and I'll be found out. And if I put it under the sofa the same thing—they'll know it couldn't have just gotten here on its own and find me out.

Then another thought turns my blood cold: What if the phone rings?

I lean my head back on the sofa, close my eyes, and try to keep from hyperventilating.

"Do you mind if I sit here?"

I open my eyes and am shocked to see Hudson Winters standing over me, his hazel eyes even more mesmerizing up close. If I was still in the other dimension I might be excited about this but now it just feels like another problem. Still, it's not like I can say no.

"Sure, of course."

"We don't have to talk or anything," he says, sitting down on the far end of the sofa and folding his arms across his chest.

Why did he even come over if he wants to ignore me? Then I realize he's probably just acting like this because the one person he knew here was killed.

"I'm sorry about your bodyguard," I say awkwardly.

"I didn't really know him, he was new, but he sure didn't deserve that," he says bitterly.

"None of them did," I say.

He doesn't say anything, just sits and looks broody. That's fine, it's not like I want to talk anyway, not when I've made this huge problem for myself. Just then I notice two agents walk in and head for the group of folding chairs. I watch them walk through the aisles, looking down as they go. Then they head back out.

"What do you think they were looking for?" I ask Hudson. My voice sounds squeaky, like I just inhaled helium.

"I don't know," he says, running his hands through his hair in this way that makes it stick up. "I guess it could be anything."

I tell myself the two agents weren't doing anything and try to respond in a normal way. "I can't believe this is happening."

"This party was supposed to be so safe my manager didn't even bother to send my usual security team," Hudson says. "He said the guy throwing the party was going to take care of it all."

"You should probably fire your manager," I say.

Hudson laughs and I find myself relaxing just the tiniest bit. Maybe it's good he sat down. I can talk to him a bit, calm down, and then figure out what to do with the phone, which has now warmed to my body temperature where it's pressed between my sweater and inner upper arm.

He leans back against the sofa. For the first time he looks more like a guy instead of a rock star. "What do you think they're going to do now that their plan got wrecked?"

"What do you mean?" I ask. I've been so obsessed with the phone I haven't even thought about anything else.

"It was Ariel and Mr. Barett they were taking out of the room," he says. "So it must have been Mr. Barett's money they were after. Now that they're dead, the guys in charge have to be scrambling to figure out how to get a paycheck for all their work. They really screwed up and they're going to have to fix it somehow."

He's right. I look at Hudson, who is frowning again, all broody. This time I have a better idea why.

"You think they'll go after you?" I ask.

He shrugs, not looking at me. "They might," he says. "They did kill my bodyguard. But I'm guessing there are people here whose parents are a lot richer than me. They could go after one of them too."

This conversation has done nothing to calm me down, in fact it's made everything worse. The one thing even more dangerous than being in a hostage situation has to be being in a hostage situation that's gone wrong. I look out the window and in the lavender hue of twilight I can see figures posted around the yard, each with a gun. What are they going to do when they realize Ariel isn't dead? I move my arm to press it against my stomach, to soothe it, but then the phone slides against my skin and suddenly I am wondering what they would do if they knew I had it. I look away from the window but panic is squeezing my lungs in an iron grip.

"Are you okay?" Hudson asks. "You're really pale. Do you want water or something?"

His concern, how genuine it is, makes me spill it. "I did something really stupid," I blurt out.

He looks surprised. "What, tonight?"

I need to keep my mouth shut and figure out what to do on my own but the panic is threatening to suffocate me and I can't keep it in. "I took a cell phone," I whisper.

"What?" Hudson's eyes darken.

"It gets worse," I say. "It's Mr. Barett's phone. It was on the floor and I picked it up a couple of minutes ago, after they collected the cell phones."

"So you have it on you now?" Hudson is looking at me like I just revealed I have a bomb strapped on under my sweater. Which is kind of what it's starting to feel like.

"I don't know what—" I begin, but I am cut off as The Assassin storms into the room. He raises his gun and fires a shot at the ceiling. A few people scream.

"Everyone over here!" The Assassin shouts, gesturing to the folding chairs.

They found out about the phone. They are going to start shooting people until they find it. Unless Hudson just stands up right now and tells them I have it. Terror feels like an animal clawing to get out of my belly.

And then I feel Hudson grab my hand. "Let's go," he says quietly.

I'm not sure my legs will hold me up but they do. The phone feels like it's burning into my arm and I turn it so that the rectangular outline isn't visible. Then we walk over and sit.

The Assassin waits until everyone is sitting, then he points the gun straight at us. "You've kept a secret from me," he says. "And I really do not like secrets."

CHAPTER 4

Ariel

I stumble backwards, whacking my head against the edge of the fireplace which hurts so much I practically see stars.

"Are you okay?" the agent asks, actually sounding concerned, which is so absurd I laugh.

This scares him—he probably thinks hitting my head made me temporarily insane.

"Why don't you sit down?" he asks, waving toward my king-sized canopy bed that looks like something out of a princess castle and totally not part of any story where people are taken hostage. When he says it he steps out of the shadow and I realize I know him. He's one of the gardeners, Milo or something. He's from some country in Central America, like the other gardeners, and he's a year or two older than me. He's not much to look at: short and muscular with thick dark hair and blunt features. He's the kind of guy you'd walk by on the street and barely even notice. I can't believe he'd backstab us like this and if he wasn't in a position to have me killed I think I'd smack him.

"I don't need your invitation to sit in my own room," I tell him. I chose every piece of furniture, the pale blue carpet, the cornflower silk bedspread and curtains, and the books piled on three different oak bookcases. He and his friends may have taken over the house but this space is still mine.

The guy laughs. "Only you would say that under such circumstances." He sounds almost admiring, with his soft accent and careful way of speaking English.

"What do you know about me?" I ask coldly.

"I work here," he says uncertainly.

"Right, before you were involved in the plot to take my birthday party hostage you were employed here," I say bitingly. "I know."

"It's not . . . " he says, faltering. "It's complicated."

I snort angrily. "They offered you more money than we did. It doesn't seem particularly complicated."

His eyes flash. "No, that's not it at all," he says, and I'm surprised by how angry he sounds. "I'm not without honor."

I roll my eyes. Who says stuff like that? "Real honorable to be part of killing an unarmed man."

It suddenly occurs to me that I should probably shut up. As far as I know the people in charge haven't realized that I'm not dead yet and Milo, or whatever his name is, is in a great position to earn some points with them by turning me in. This is my problem; whenever I'm angry, which is a lot, I say whatever I feel like saying instead of thinking through actual consequences.

But Milo shakes his head, his eyes suddenly going soft. "It was a terrible accident," he says, real sorrow in his voice. "I'm so sorry for your loss."

"Hard to swallow that when you're part of the whole thing," I tell him.

I walk over to my desk and lean against it. This desk used to belong to my grandmother—it's an old-fashioned roll top with all these compartments and little drawers and I love it.

"It wasn't my choice," he says, his eyes pleading with me to believe him. "I would never be part of something like this if I weren't being forced. And I'm not going to hurt anyone, no matter what."

"Whatever," I say.

"I would never hurt you or anyone else in this house," he repeats.

"Tell that to my dad and Bianca," I say, the words biting into me. I look away for a moment and when I look back he is staring at me, his eyes shining with sympathy I don't want.

"Truly, I am sorry," he says, in his formal way.

His gaze is practically melty. I sigh irritably. Of course. He has a crush on me. I'm guessing he's had it for a while, totally not bothered that it's a complete cliché to be into your rich boss's blond daughter. I should be thankful though. His pathetic crush on the person he imagines me to be is probably what's going to keep him from turning me in.

"How did you get here?" he asks, looking at the fireplace behind me.

I so don't want him to find out about the tunnels but a moment later he's looking in. "Wow," he says when he backs out. "Do these go all over the house?"

"Just between a couple of rooms," I say. "It's not a big deal."

"But it saved your life."

"Yeah, that part is cool," I admit.

"I won't tell anyone about it," he says, so earnestly I have to look away.

I don't know if I believe him but it's not like there's anything I can do about it either way.

"So who's the mastermind behind this takeover?" I ask, deciding to see if he can be useful to me.

He laughs, a surprisingly jolly sound. "I am a grunt, not someone trusted with information. I don't even know what happens past this shift."

"What's your shift?" I ask. Anything he can tell me could turn out to be useful.

"We all monitor different segments of the house," he says. "I'm to be covering the upstairs study, your room, the bathroom, and hallway, being on the lookout for anything unusual."

"So what are you doing hanging out in my bedroom?" I ask, arching a brow.

His tan cheeks begin to turn a dusty rose, which amuses me. "I was thinking about you," he admits. "You always seemed so sad and to die alone like that just seemed wrong."

My head snaps back as though his words were a slap across my face. How dare he make assumptions about my life. Especially assumptions that are spot on.

"I was hardly alone," I sniff. "I was with my best friends." And my father but I'm not going to say his name again.

Milo shakes his head. "Those people are not your friends," he says, all serious and wise and incredibly annoying.

"What do you know about it?"

His cheeks begin to turn pink again. "Nothing, I'm sorry."

He's like the kind of guy who would write love poems and cultivate roses, not take part in a hostage situation. Actually he does cultivate beautiful roses, though I bet any poems he writes are drowning in clichés. In any case, I am done with this conversation.

"Can you give me some privacy?" I ask.

Milo runs a hand through his thick black hair. "Yes, but you should not stay here long," he says. "Once they find out you are alive they will hunt you."

That word makes a shiver travel across my skin. "I'll be careful."

"I am here if you need me." With one final, soulful glance, he is gone.

I let out a sigh and collapse on my bed, the goose down of my comforter cuddling me. I know I need to think about Abby and my uncle and what to do next but for one second I close my eyes and just breathe.

Then suddenly, from downstairs, I hear shots.

CHAPTER 5

Sera

The room is dead silent as The Assassin pauses. The bright light hurts my eyes, or maybe it's the lingering smell of gunpowder, smoky with a hint of salt. Or maybe it's the phone, which feels like it is going to sear my skin off.

"We have learned that Ariel is not the girl who was killed," The Assassin says, his voice iced fury. "Something that you knew but chose not to tell us. And now she is somewhere in this house and we must find her, which is your opportunity to make up for your mistake. Who here can help us with that?"

I am suddenly able to breathe for the first time since The Assassin came in. He's not after the phone! At least not yet. But then his words fully sink in and my belly feels heavy, like it's full of stones. I know where Ariel is, at least I think I do, but how can I say anything? To do so would be as bad as picking up a gun and killing her myself. I hate her but obviously not in a murder kind of way.

The Assassin walks toward the first row of chairs and pauses at Mike Schmidt, a soccer star who's probably the biggest guy in the room after Hudson. Mike has blond hair that he wears long, European style, and it's usually artfully arranged, even when he's tearing down the field. But now it's falling in his face, which is red, his eyes darting around like a trapped animal.

The Assassin reaches out and grabs Mike so fast I gasp.

"Where is she?" The Assassin demands. His face is close to Mike's, the gun pressed against Mike's chest.

"I don't know," Mike squeaks, a sound I've never heard him make.

I am nauseous.

"Are you sure?" The Assassin shoves him and he stumbles. The Assassin raises the gun and releases the safety, cocking it like he is about to shoot Mike.

People gasp, a few girls cover their faces. I think my heart has officially stopped beating.

"I don't know anything, I swear," Mike says, tears making his voice ragged.

The Assassin reaches for him again, this time shoving him back toward the seats. Mike falls wordlessly into a chair and puts his face in his hands. I exhale loudly, my chest light again. Hudson squeezes my hand and I can't believe how reassuring the tiny gesture is.

The Assassin watches Mike for a moment, then whips around and presses the gun to Cassidy's head. "What about you? What can you tell us about your missing friend?"

"Nothing," Cassidy says.

She is extremely polite and her eyes are downcast, but she's not terrified in the way Mike was, or the way I'd be if that gun was pointed at me. Cassidy is made of tougher stock than the rest of us. Her father is a senator who weathered not one but two political scandals that crucified the entire family in the national press. I guess if you can get through that when you're ten and twelve, a few armed agents aren't going to scare you.

"I mean, it's Ariel's house so she probably knows hiding places we don't," she adds.

"But you've been here before, no?" he asks, gun aimed at her temple.

"Yes, I think most of us have," Cassidy says. "But we just hang out and watch movies or go swimming. I don't know anywhere she'd hide. If I did I would tell you."

She would, for sure.

The Assassin seems to be able to tell this as well because he lowers the gun.

But then Cassidy speaks again. "You should ask Sera," she says, looking over at me with a silky smile. "She used to play here when she was a kid and she knows this house better than any of us."

I freeze as my classmates turn to look back at me. My heart is in my throat, threatening to choke me.

"Sera, stand," The Assassin orders, lifting the gun.

I stand, light-headed and trembling. I feel like a spotlight is shining on my left arm where the phone is hidden and I press it against my body, praying that now is not the moment it rings. I don't even realize that Hudson still has my hand until he squeezes it, hard. He's not letting go.

"What can you tell me?" The Assassin asks.

Tears swim in my eyes. He's barely even pointing the gun at me; I guess he can tell he doesn't have to, I scare easy. But despite what Cassidy said, I don't backstab, not like this.

"I don't, I mean, I don't know," I babble. I have to say *something*. "There are closets and stuff obviously. And like there's an attic. You could hide behind boxes and stuff up there I think."

The Assassin nods curtly. "Attic," he says with a wave of his hand, and two of the agents take off. "Anything else?"

I shake my head.

He pauses for a moment, then lowers the gun to one shoulder. "Let me urge you all to think long and hard," he says coldly. "Anyplace she might be, any way she might try to escape, anything at all that occurs to you, let us know." He looks at me. "And anyone who helps her will be shot." He gives a flick of his wrist and walks out, most of the agents following behind.

The few agents left spread out, guns held loosely in their hands. My body sags in relief. I don't even realize that I'm leaning against Hudson until he shifts slightly.

"Sorry," I say, sitting back up.

"That was intense. Are you okay?"

"I don't even know what that means right now." My voice is still unsteady.

Sweat is running down my arms and I'm worried it will make the phone slippery. Plus I just realized what I should have said: the basement of the garage, which is actually some kind of bomb shelter a former owner had built in the fifties. You can only get to it through a panel in the floor and if you don't know it's there, you'd think it was just a slightly misaligned floorboard. That would have kept them off her trail longer.

"Did you slash that girl's tires or something?" Hudson asks, looking at Cassidy. "Because she has it in for you."

"That she does."

"So the phone," he says softly.

I shake my head. "Can we not talk about that yet? I just need a minute of not thinking about life-threatening things."

Hudson nods, then looks around the room. Most of my classmates have migrated back to the sofas and chairs outside the study. They sit close together, some with arms around each other, others sitting on the floor and resting against someone's legs. They talk in low voices, heads bent toward each other, supporting and comforting each other.

"This reminds me of going home," he says.

"What?" I ask, so thankful for the change in topic that I could hug him.

He nods toward my classmates. "This kind of loathing. This is how my brothers and sisters act when I make the mistake of coming home. They want to make sure I don't forget how much they hate me."

"Why do they hate you so much?" I ask. And then something else occurs to me. "I thought you were an only child."

I've read enough about Hudson to know he grew up in a Boston suburb, the only child of a baker.

He smiles a bitter smile. "That would be your answer. I sold my soul to the gods of the record companies and changed my past."

"So you're not the only son of a baker from Newton?" I ask. I can almost forget the phone in my curiosity. Almost.

"I'm the son of an unemployed coal miner from Appalachia," he says, rubbing his thumb against his face for a moment. "And the youngest of seven very pissed off siblings."

"What's the big deal? I mean, who cares where you're from when you can sing like you do."

"It was bad advice," he says simply, looking down at his hands. "My first manager thought it would make me more appealing. By the time I actually got good managers, people who would have made my story sound like some kind of living fairy tale, I was already stuck in the lie."

"So now it's the lie that matters, not what your past actually was." I realize that's probably why he comes across as such a snob in interviews: He's lying.

"Yup," he says. "That's my big secret, not that I'm a poor kid from Appalachia but that I'm a liar. And there's no spinning that one to make it a fairy tale."

I think about this for a minute. "You're really trapped," I say, feeling bad for him.

"Kind of like we are right now in this house. Except you have something that might help us." He leans forward, those hazel eyes staring at me intently. "So now that I told you my secret, trust me and let's use that phone."

Of course this was where it was going. He's smart because calculated or not, him telling me his secret really does make me trust him more.

Hudson is looking at me steadily. "That phone is our ticket out of here."

"It would be if we could use it," I point out. "They monitor us everywhere."

Hudson considers. "There has to be a way we can check out if it works. Let's go back over to the sofa and sit so you're facing the wall."

"But it's practically out in the open. An agent could see us. And that guy said anyone with a phone will be shot and two other people too. It's too big a risk." I cast around for other ideas. "Won't there be someone checking up on you, seeing how the concert went? Maybe when they can't get in touch they'll send the police to see what's going on."

Hudson shakes his head, his expression rueful. "I don't get checked up on after concerts. That's when I need downtime, not babysitting. My manager learned that lesson long ago. So unless your parents or someone else's decide to check in early . . ."

I slump back against the cushions. "Not likely." There's no reason for anyone to assume there's anything wrong, not when we were invited to a weekend-long party with nonstop fun planned the entire time.

"So we're back to the phone," Hudson says. "I get that it's a risk but what choice do we have? This situation has already started to go south and we need to do anything we can to get out of here, before it gets worse."

I know he's right but I so don't want to do this. I don't want to be brave and risk my life trying to make a secret call. But it seems so cowardly to say that and really, why did I pick up the phone if I wasn't somehow thinking about using it?

So I follow him and sit down so that I am facing the wall, Hudson across from me.

"Where is it?" he whispers.

I turn my arm just so he can see the outline against my sweater.

"Okay, just slide it out and pass it to me," he says. "Or do you want to try and text 911?"

I am thinking random things, like is it even possible to text 911 and wondering if my sweat might have broken the phone. But I still manage to slip it out from my sleeve, my skin warm where I had it pressed for so long, and it rests on the sofa between us. I pull it close to my body, then pull my knees up so unless you are sitting on one of our laps or standing right above us, you can't see it.

For a moment we just stare at it, a small black rectangle with a shimmery top.

"He probably had it on vibrate, right?" Hudson asks. "Because of the concert?"

He's right. Mr. Barett would never turn the phone off but he'd have put it on vibrate for his daughter's birthday concert. I wish I'd thought of that earlier so I wasn't panicked it might ring.

"I'll cough just in case," I say.

I take a deep breath, let out a short cough and stab the on button at the same time. The screen lights up soundlessly and Hudson grins at me.

"Awesome," he says.

He sounds as joyful as I feel and for a second I can already see the police streaming in, The Assassin being led off in handcuffs, Ariel coming out of hiding, and all of us living happily ever after. Or at least getting to go home.

But then we look down at the screen. It's a soothing midnight blue with the words "please enter code." It's like getting punched in the chest.

Because after all this, the phone is completely and totally useless.

CHAPTER 6

Ariel

I am on the floor of the tunnel, far enough from the living room grate that I'm not worried about being seen but close enough that light from the chandelier creates faint shadows on my dress. I was so sure The Assassin was going to shoot Mike or Cassidy—I still can't believe they're alive. But they're in danger. When I fled here, into the tunnels, I wasn't thinking about that. My disappearance has made the agents angry and they were already capable of murder back when things were going their way. I don't want to know what they're capable of now. And Sera didn't tell them where I was though she has to know. Or did she just forget about the tunnels like she forgot about what it means not to be a backstabbing traitor?

Whatever, I'm not going to waste time thinking about her now. Uncle Marc is going to be here soon and if I can get to him before the agents do, he can get help and stop Abby from coming here. It's a long shot but the one thing I have on my side is surprise: They won't know he's coming. I head back toward the stairs. I'll go to my room and change into something more practical than my short pink party dress, something dark that will help me hide in shadows and allow me to move quickly. I should have done it before but Milo was there. Then I'll see if there's any way I can get up to the roof, to the helicopter pad where Uncle Marc will be coming in. It's probably too much to hope that a helicopter could land unnoticed, but maybe I can hide on the roof and figure out something.

I am close to my room when I hear the noise. Glass shattering, something falling on the floor, drawers being opened, more stuff falling on the floor.

The light is on in my room and I see movement. I tiptoe up as quietly as I can, then have to cover my mouth to keep from gasping out loud. They are ransacking my room.

My china lamp, the one that's been in my family for generations, is in shards on the floor, the bits getting crunched as agents step on them. Every drawer has been taken out of my beautiful desk and overturned, several cracked down the middle in the process. My computer is long gone but now my papers are being spread about, read, then tossed on the floor. The little keepsakes I had on the desk and my dresser—the princess drawing Abby sent me last week and the photo of the junior class trip to Paris and the tiny Eiffel Tower Bianca gave me as a joke—are being crushed underfoot. We almost left it at the café we went to after the Eiffel Tower but at the last minute I remembered and went back for it. Now it's in jagged shards on my floor. Someone is actually slicing my powder-blue armchair and stuffing is flying everywhere. Clothes are being pulled out of my dresser and tossed on the floor. Someone else is going through my jewelry box, slipping bracelets and necklaces—some of the only things my mother left me—into his or her pockets.

My stomach heaves and for a moment I worry I might throw up. It's just stuff but seeing it manhandled like this makes me feel naked and violated. And angry. These people are animals.

Then I notice one person doing what he can to quell the damage. He is picking up keepsakes, placing drawers back carefully, putting clothes back on hangers. It's Milo of course. For a moment I just feel scornful—what difference does it make if my clothes are wrinkled or he keeps the Eiffel Tower from being broken into even more pieces. But I have to admit there is something soothing about seeing him do what he can to protect my things. He may be annoying but he's also a nice guy, the kind of guy who ends up crushed like my lamp, with people grinding their heels in as they walk right over it. But seeing him now I realize that if I need it, he will help me.

And before this night is through I may well need it.

I back away from my room. My uncle is coming in less than an hour and I need to be waiting for him. I walk away from the sounds of destruction, closing it off from my mind. It's done so what does it matter? All that concerns me now is what's going to happen next.

CHAPTER 7

Sera

We can't break the code. I mean, we've only been trying for about ten minutes but I've used everything I can think of: Mr. Barett's birthday, his anniversary with Ariel's mom, our zip code, his cell phone number. I can think of a lot of other things it might be, like the zip code from his hometown, Pittsburgh, or the license plate of his first car, but without using the Internet on the phone, I can't find out what those things are. And we're trying to be as subtle as possible, though the agents are mostly staying in the doorways, not coming close enough to see what we're doing.

"This sucks," I say through clenched teeth after the numerals that correspond to the name Barett fail.

"Let's take a break," Hudson says. "Sometimes what you're looking for doesn't pop into your head until you stop looking for it."

I let out my breath in a frustrated rush. Maybe he's right. I slip the phone back up my sleeve. I wish I'd worn looser pants so I could put it in a pocket. "Is that what you do when you're writing songs?"

He smiles. "Yeah, it is. I think about something totally different, like if I'm writing about a breakup I go online and check football scores."

That makes me smile. "So what totally different thing should we talk about?"

He glances at my classmates, all fifteen of them hanging out together. "Tell me why everyone in your class hates you."

The words sting, though of course he's noticed. It's not possible to miss. "I think I'd rather drive myself crazy thinking about the code."

He laughs but then looks at me, waiting.

I take a deep breath. What does it matter if I tell him?

"Last spring break Ariel and her dad went to Mexico," I begin. "And while they were there this group of guys attacked Ariel."

It doesn't sound so bad when I just say the words. It didn't even sound that bad when she texted me about it, after the fact, when she was in the airport coming home. She said they had just broken into her hotel room and started hitting her when they were caught, so it seemed like maybe it was scary but not that big a deal, at least not when you figured they were there to rape and maybe even kill her.

But then she came home and I saw her.

"They beat her up," I say. "Bad." Her eyes were both purple, the flesh around them spongy and swollen. There were scratches on her face and neck that she couldn't hide with makeup, no matter how much she put on, and greenish-brown bruises on the insides of her arms. "But that wasn't even the worst part. It did something to her. It was like you'd look in her eyes and no one was there. She started being destructive, cutting school and picking fights with anyone she could."

"It sounds like she had some kind of posttraumatic stress syndrome," Hudson says. "That happened to my brother who was in the Army."

I nod. "Yeah, that's what the psychiatrist said."

"So at least she was getting help."

"No," I say, the word a rock in the soft part of my belly. "She didn't want help. She kept saying she was over it, not to worry. I practically begged her to tell someone what was going on but she wouldn't and she made me swear I wouldn't."

I kept my promise too, until the day I saw that she had been taking a razor and slicing up her inner arms, harsh red lines across the pale skin.

"I told the counselor at our school," I said. "And they reported it and all these social workers came to her house and she had to go to a facility" (mental institution but I can't say those words) "and have mandated therapy."

"And I take it Ariel didn't appreciate you doing that."

The first couple of days I knew she'd be mad but then I figured she'd see my side, know that I did it to help. I was so wrong.

"You have no idea," I tell him, staring out the window.

Hudson reaches across the sofa and rests his hand on my shoulder. I'm shocked that even under these conditions I feel a tingle from his touch.

"You did the right thing," he says.

That's what my parents said, and John Avery once he got involved. But they didn't see the fury in Ariel, the hatred that radiated whenever she came within ten feet of me. And how fast she turned everyone against me.

"You don't believe me," he says.

"I think if it was the right thing she would have forgiven me by now."

He shakes his head. "That's not how it works." He sighs. "But I hear you."

He does. And it feels kind of good to be heard after all these months of being invisible. But now I'm done talking about this. "I'm starving," I say, stretching a little but being careful the arm with the phone stays facing the wall. "Do you think we can get something to eat?"

"It's worth a try," Hudson says, standing up.

We walk toward the doorway that leads to the hallway to the kitchen. An agent is standing in the doorway and he moves to block us from going by.

"Um, is it okay to get something to eat?" Hudson asks.

"No," the agent says. "There's going to be a search and no one leaves this room until it's over."

A bad feeling begins in the center of my chest. "What kind of search?" I ask.

The agent shrugs. "Something went missing in here. The agents are taking each one of you into a room and searching you."

I think I might puke.

"Okay," Hudson says, taking my arm and leading me back to the sofa where I practically collapse.

"They want the cell phone," I whisper frantically.

"We don't know that," he says, but he has a cornered look in his eyes.

"We do. I saw agents looking for it before. They were walking around the area where Mr. Barett was shot, looking on the ground for something. It has to be the phone."

Hudson lets out a long breath and runs his hands through his hair, making it stick up. I have a sudden and inappropriate urge to smooth it.

I look over at my classmates and now there are only fourteen. I look through them and realize that Ella is the one being searched. I cringe inwardly at the thought of any of the agents touching any of us.

"What are we going to do?" I ask him. "We can't just leave it in the sofa for someone to find."

Hudson is looking over my shoulder and I look in that direction, past where my classmates are sitting, to the doorway of the study. Ella is being walked out by an agent, her face all scrunched. When she sits down Mike puts his arm around her. The agent points to Franz Collet, who says something as he stands, something that angers the agent I guess because he punches Franz, hard.

A sound echoes around the room as Franz falls back on the sofa, crying out in pain. Blood is pouring down his face and his hands cover his nose, his eyes shiny with tears from the blow.

"Get up!" the agent shouts at Franz, towering menacingly over him.

Franz struggles to his feet and the agent grabs his arm, then twists it behind him and shoves him toward the doorway. Blood is still flowing down Franz's face and his arm is bent at an impossible angle behind his back as the agent continues to manhandle him out of the room.

Then the door shuts and Franz is gone. The room is eerily silent in his wake.

After a moment one of the agents standing in the doorway to the living room clears his throat and speaks. "Your friend forgot who was in charge," he says coolly. "I suggest you don't make the same mistake."

Obviously I didn't hear what Franz said but I do know he'd never challenge the agent, that I'm sure of. Really none of us would do anything to challenge them, we're not stupid. I look at Hudson whose dismay mirrors my own.

"He didn't have to hit Franz," I say softly, my stomach queasy.

"I know," Hudson says, glancing at the agent who spoke, then looking away. "They don't want us to forget for a second who has the power."

People are starting to talk again, quietly, and I see the agents slouch back against the doorways. Before I'd seen that as a sign of being relaxed but now it feels more like they are snakes, coiled and still, but ready to lash out at the slightest provocation.

"It was mean," I say.

Hudson looks amused and I realize how stupid it sounds to call machine-gun-toting hostage-holders mean.

"You know what I'm saying. We know they're in charge, they don't have to go beating us up to prove it."

"They don't have to but they can and they will if they want to," Hudson says. "That's what they're really reminding us." He lets out a long breath and then presses his hands together. "But we don't have time to worry about it now. We have to figure out what to do with the phone." He glances toward the agents when he says it, his voice even lower than before.

My stomach rolls over in a nauseating swirl. I would do anything to be able to undo having picked up this stupid, useless phone.

"This is what I'm thinking," he says softly. "We'll put the phone under one of the sofa cushions while they search us. Then the first one of us out gets it and hides it in our clothing. It should be safe to hold onto it once they've finished searching us."

I want to point out how flawed this is as a plan but I don't because what else are we going to do? "Thanks," I say instead.

His eyebrows wrinkle. "For what, coming up with a pretty half-assed plan?"

I grin but then I shake my head. "For helping me with this. It doesn't have to be your problem. I'm the one who took the phone." Something occurs to me and even though it's stupid, I have to know. "Why did you come over to me? I mean, out of everyone here, why me?"

The corner of his mouth pulls up in a half grin. "Because you were the one who laughed at my joke."

When he introduced himself as Hunter, making fun of Mr. Barett who had messed up his name. It's ridiculous when our lives are in the balance but I have a warm glow from his words. I felt so dumb being the only one who laughed but he liked it.

"Oh," I say, trying to sound nonchalant but failing pretty badly.

He nods but doesn't say anything because the agent is heading over to us. My glow is replaced by clammy panic as I stuff my arm in between the seat cushions, let the phone slide out and pull my hand back out.

"You," the agent says, pointing at me.

I stand on legs that feel like liquid, and follow him into the study.

CHAPTER 8

Ariel

I spent twenty minutes in the guest office making a sign for Marc. In big, black letters it explains that we are being held hostage, that he needs to get away and call 911. My plan was to hold up the sign when the helicopter got close; he'd read it, follow the directions, and we'd be free within the hour, long before Abby would ever get near the house. It was a perfect plan: simple, easy, and foolproof.

But then came the problem: I can't figure out how to get to the roof. I've been crawling through the tunnels like a rat in a maze and finally realized the only ways to the roof are from outside the house and from the office wing my dad put on the house. There are no hidden back stairs like I'd hoped, which means not only is there no way to get to the roof from the tunnels, there's no exit from the tunnels anywhere near the stairs up to the helicopter landing pad. I'd have to go through my dad's offices and those are teeming with agents whom I assume are trying to figure out how to use Abby and Uncle Marc instead of me and my dad to get their money.

I'm sitting on the floor by the hallway grate closest to his offices, seething, the stupid sign useless next to me. And with way too much time to think about the thing I most don't want to think about: Sera. What happened in the living room is like a fish hook in my mind. She has to know where I am. We spent hours in these tunnels, practically lived in them the year we were ten. Yes, she forgot a lot but there's no forgetting something like that. She knows where I am and she didn't say. Which is a new thing for her—she's not got a good track record for keeping her mouth shut.

For about the billionth time I feel the surge of hot rage at the center of my belly for what she did, like a furnace blast roasting my insides. My so-called best friend essentially got me put in the loony bin, on the lock-down ward, stripped of my belt and shoelaces for forty-eight hours, until I finally managed to reach John Avery and get out.

But much worse than being in the mental ward was that people found out. The one way I had managed to keep it together was to pretend Mexico had never happened. But thanks to Sera I had to talk about it. It took everything in me not to become a pathetic mound of quivering emotional jelly on the floor of New Canaan Country Day every day.

Hating Sera helped keep me solid, as did my disdain for anyone who tried to sympathize. People learned fast. They also learned not to talk to Sera, though social death felt like much too soft a price for her to pay. If she'd just let it go, the way I asked her, I know I'd be past it now. It's her fault I still wake up in a cold sweat almost every night, my body clammy, my heart slamming around in my chest, the metallic taste of fear coating my tongue.

But even that wasn't the worst part.

I hear voices that shake me out of the past, back to the hard floor of the tunnel, but they are too far away to make out actual words. I look at my watch, the dial lit up and telling me it's 8:58. Uncle Marc's helicopter is closing in and there's absolutely nothing I can do to warn him or to get him to help Abby. I want to scream in frustration.

I hear footsteps and I stand up, lean closer to the grate, and peer out. Two agents have John trapped between them. They speak in low voices, the words "still make it work" come through in a whisper but I can't see their faces, only the backs of their heads so I don't know who is speaking. I think it might be better that I can't hear everything they say because it would probably make me feel worse than I already do, sitting here useless.

Their voices fade as they move farther away and I suddenly remember my twelfth birthday. That one was a sleepover with all the girls in my class. At the last minute my dad couldn't make it home from a meeting in Chicago so John stepped in to chaperone.

He made sure the pizza came on time and he even joined us for dessert, make-your-own sundaes. He didn't stop me when I poured on a gallon of caramel sauce, or tell me "I told you so" when I got a stomachache later. He also didn't tell my dad when a game of Truth or Dare got out of hand and Julia Smith hit her head diving into the pool. We got her out fast and she was fine but my dad would have flipped out over liability. John just made sure everyone was okay and suggested we take the game inside. He's always been cool like that.

I hear the sound of a door shutting, steps, and voices, and I lean my face against the grate again. In a great rush a knot of agents swoops past. At the center, I see a Yankees cap set unevenly over a head of very red hair: Uncle Marc.

The last time I saw him was last month when he came over after my dad's lawyer's funeral. Mr. Black was killed in a car accident and my dad was really upset about it. He sat alone in the living room doing shots of whiskey in the dark until Marc got him reminiscing about Steelers games they went to when they were kids, sometimes sneaking in. That cheered my dad up, at least enough that he didn't drink himself into a stupor. That's the thing about Marc, he makes everything better.

My chest tightens at the site of my goofy uncle as he is whisked by. I catch only a quick glimpse of his face and see how somber he looks, an expression that's totally out of place for him, the eternal kid who is always smiling about something. I don't think he is going to be able to make this better.

A feeling is snaking its way around my stomach, through my chest. It brings with it the smell of Windex and lemon, the smell at the hotel in Mexico. As always I am powerless as it winds its way around my insides, paralyzing me.

It's not the memory of the guys breaking into my room that makes my throat tighten like a gloved hand is wrapping around it, squeezing. It's not how they shouted, how one held me while another punched me again and again. And it's not how they tied me up, put a bag over my head, and threw me on the floor like a sack of garbage.

Yes, those things were awful. But they don't touch the feeling that came with the force of a wave grabbing me and pulling me underwater so fast it crushed me: the feeling of pure and total helplessness. There are no words for that feeling, knowing that they could do anything to me, anything they wanted, and there was nothing I could do to stop it. *I* was nothing, just a whimpering, pleading bundle of nothing. Thinking of my begging makes me want to heave. But remembering that helplessness makes me feel dead. Which was why I was slicing my arm. I wasn't trying to kill myself, I was just trying to feel alive again.

Knowing that John and now Marc are trapped in this, and knowing that Abby is going to be dropped off and there's nothing I can do to stop it, is massing together into another wave about to engulf me.

I struggle to my feet, my stomach heaving, and run back to my room, pausing just long enough to make sure it's empty. I race in and make it to the bathroom just in time. I sink in front of the toilet and the contents of my stomach come rushing up, bile stinging my throat. I puke and puke and puke, every last drop in my stomach pumping out of me. I'm not even aware of the hand smoothing back my hair until I stop, spent and empty on the cool tile.

"Are you okay?" It's Milo.

I can't talk yet, my throat is too raw so I just nod.

"I heard the noise in here," he says. "But I don't think anyone else did."

In a minute I'll care about that and be thankful that it was him and not another agent who came to check things out in my room. In a minute my stomach will settle and my throat won't be burning. And in a minute I will stand up and do something. I need to act, to stop thinking and move, to interfere with what is happening in my house.

Because I will die before I'll ever be that helpless again.

CHAPTER 9

Sera

It was just a pat down. I mean, it was more thorough than you'd want but not a strip search or anything, and it was obviously a woman so it definitely wasn't what it could have been. I feel relieved about this for about ten seconds, then start my phone panic again. But Hudson is still on the sofa so no one could have found it while I was gone.

The agent leads me to my seat, then points to Hudson when we reach our sofa oasis. I watch for a second as they go, then as subtly as I can, slip my fingers between the seat cushions and nestle the phone back up my sleeve. It's starting to feel like it's part of my body. I try to brainstorm more code possibilities but I don't try any of them out, not while there's a room search coming and Hudson isn't here to keep watch while I do it. It's not like I come up with anything good anyway.

Hudson is back about five minutes later and he grins as he gets closer. "The agent said we can eat something now."

That is the best news I've heard in a while.

He gives me an inquiring look about the phone and I nod.

"Let's go," he says, leading the way across the huge room. We both slow down as we get closer to the doorway where an agent stands, gun at his side.

"Um, we were told it's okay to go to the kitchen to get something to eat," Hudson says. I see him picking at his fingernail as he speaks.

The agent nods and waves us through. My legs feel a little shaky as we walk down the short hall to the kitchen.

The Barett kitchen is amazing: wide expanses of granite countertop, gleaming Le Creuset cookwear hanging from racks, state-of-the-art appliances that are so sleek they have a sports car feel to them. A skylight opens the ceiling and when I look up I see stars far off in the night sky.

If it weren't for the agents lurking in both doorways it would almost feel normal.

The agent at the far doorway sees us come in. "You can eat what's on the counter or stuff from the fridge," she says. "No opening drawers or cabinets. Got it?"

We both nod. The huge island in the middle of the room is covered with trays of hors d'oeurvre.

"Should we heat some of these up?" I ask, looking at the shrimp toast and mini-quiches. My stomach is a tangle of knots and I'm not sure how much I'll actually be able to eat.

Hudson grabs a goat cheese and bacon roll and stuffs it in his mouth, looking like any of the guys I go to school with scarfing down a hamburger. I guess refinement doesn't come with fame.

"This is okay to start but I want real food," he says. "Not just stuff to graze on."

"I hear that."

It's Mike and he's walking in with Trevor, Ravi, and Ella. Ella stopped talking to me when everyone else did, of course, but she lent me clothes after gym once, when mine mysteriously disappeared from my locker, and she's one of the only girls who never sent me dirty looks or started whispering when I walked in the room in those awful early weeks. Obviously she's not a friend—I don't have any of those—but she's not an enemy either. I sit on one of the stools, my arm resting across my lap, hiding the phone as the agent repeats the kitchen rules. I can eat with my other hand, if I can manage to choke something down.

"Where's the meat?" Trevor asks, opening the fridge.

He is striving to sound jovial but his eyes are darting around, as though on the lookout for an agent to come haul him away. I guess we're all kind of feeling that way.

"I think Ariel said it was going to be sushi for dinner," Ella says, and all three guys groan.

"There has to at least be sandwich stuff in here," Trevor says, poking around in the huge fridge.

"What happened to serving steak?" Mike asks, peering over Trevor's shoulder. "Because that's a dinner."

He is doing a better job of sounding normal but I think he's looked at the clock like ten times in the two minutes he's been in here. I would know—I keep checking it myself.

"A real dinner is barbeque," Hudson says, grabbing a wedge of brie. Even his voice has the undercurrent of tension we are all feeling.

Ravi glances at Hudson, his face slightly flushed. All the guys are talking just a bit too loudly and not quite looking at Hudson. I realize they are starstruck, which is kind of funny because they usually walk around like rock stars themselves. It's also strange to realize that I stopped thinking about Hudson as a rock star hours ago.

Ravi takes a mini spring roll and eats it. "These aren't bad," he says, his voice just slightly higher than usual.

Ravi is one of those guys who gets off on risk, who does every extreme sport there is, and who's broken like twelve bones. The fact that his face is tight, that his hands are shaky, makes the knots in my stomach tighten.

"Sweet potato biscuits are better," Hudson says to me with a grin.

It's almost like he knows I need distraction. Though I'm probably reading too much into it, he's probably just starving and excited to eat.

Ella raises her eyebrows and I see the guys exchange looks. I guess they're surprised that of anyone he could talk to, Hudson chose me. I mean, if I hadn't told him about the phone who knows if we'd still be hanging out, but they don't know that.

The agent in the doorway shifts and we all glance over. The knots in my stomach tighten but I guess she was just stretching because she doesn't say anything. Still, the air in the room feels different. Ella clears her throat and Trevor pulls out a sushi tray.

"I guess we'll just bring this out," he says.

The three of them head out, Ella casting one last look at Hudson, then a bleaker glance at the agents.

"I bet I can find something in here," Hudson says, walking over to the fridge.

I pick up a stalk of endive with blue cheese and shaved apple. I'm curious what Hudson will come up with but I still feel too anxious to think about eating very much.

"Victory," he says happily, emerging from the fridge with a yellow plastic package.

He clearly doesn't have the same problem. What is it with guys and food?

I stifle a laugh when I realize what he's holding.

"That's Mr. Barett's guilty pleasure," I say.

But as soon as I say his name there's a weird hollowness in my stomach. Because Mr. Barett will never eat a midnight baloney sandwich again.

"I thank him for it," Hudson says.

I hear a noise in the doorway and we turn again. Another agent has arrived and the two of them start talking in low voices. For a few moments I wait, to see if there's some kind of problem, but it seems like they're just passing time. Which is actually kind of a relief because I don't feel quite as watched.

"All the gourmet food here and you're really going to eat baloney?" I ask Hudson.

"Baloney is quality food," he says, as he pulls on the package. It's hard to open without a utensil but he manages.

"I can think of a lot of food experts who would dispute that," I say.

"They'd be dead wrong." He flashes me a grin. "I'm making you a sandwich too."

He is back at the fridge taking out lettuce, mayo, sliced cheddar, and a loaf of bread. I watch him for a moment, then notice the vase of lilacs resting on the side of the counter. I reach out and run my hand over one feathery bloom.

"You like lilacs?" Hudson asks, laying slices of cheese on the bread.

"They're my favorite," I say, leaning in to inhale their heavenly scent. It feels so good to stop thinking about the agents and Ariel and everything going on around us. I know it won't last but I wish it could.

Hudson whips up the sandwiches, slathering an appalling amount of mayo on the bread (which he spreads with a folded piece of bread because we can't open a drawer for a knife), and piling each sandwich with towers of baloney. He adds lettuce and with a flourish of triumph, passes me mine on one of the small plates piled up next to the trays of food.

I look at it unsure how to start. It looks way too big to bite as is. "I think I might need a fork or something."

Hudson scoffs. "You rich folks and your crazy ideas," he says, wrapping his hands around his sandwich. "It's simple. It's a sandwich and you eat it with your hands."

"You're rich," I point out.

His face seems to crumple the tiniest bit. "I guess."

I think about the fact that his money was earned on a lie and how much that clearly bothers him. I can think of a hundred people who couldn't care less how their families got rich. And I realize I like the fact that he *does* care.

"So are you going to show me how to eat this thing or what?" I ask.

He grins and then defying both odds and gravity he manages to get the thing into his mouth and takes a huge bite.

I carefully pick up my sandwich. A slice of baloney slithers out the back but I get the rest of it up and stuff as much as I can into my mouth.

"There you go," Hudson says approvingly, his mouth full.

I chew. Hudson's right—baloney really *is* good.

He smiles at me. "You love it."

There's no denying it as I take another bite, a bit of mayo dribbling down my chin which I quickly wipe away.

We eat in companionable silence for a few minutes. I plan to only eat half of my sandwich; I gave up carbs a year ago and processed food when I was eleven. But if there was ever a time to break food rules, it's when you're being held hostage and could get shot at any minute for having a cell phone.

When I'm done I lean back and groan. "That was incredible but I think my stomach might explode."

"That is one of the dangers of baloney," Hudson says, putting both our plates in the sink. He does it naturally, like he's just some regular guy trained by his mom, not someone so rich he can have people wait on him hand and foot. "Do you think they have—"

A sharp voice interrupts him. "Everyone come to the living room."

I realize I've been lulled by our conversation, allowed myself to forget for just a few minutes what's going on around us. But now a third agent appears in the doorway and she sounds serious. I stand up, my body tensing.

"Now," she says.

The sandwich is turning into a ball of cement in my stomach and Hudson's cheeks have lost their reddish hue. He looks pale under the lights as I follow him out of the kitchen and back to the living room where The Assassin is telling everyone to sit. My classmates are mostly there, sitting up straight as though we are about to take a final. It's funny to think that less than twenty-four hours ago finals were our biggest worry.

"We haven't found Ariel," The Assassin says, his words clipped. "Which can only mean one thing. You helped her or you're helping her now, keeping her concealed from us. She is somewhere on the property, that we know for sure, and so I'll ask one more time. Where is Ariel?"

A terrible silence follows. I put my hands on my bloated stomach, afraid I might puke.

"You need more incentive I see," The Assassin says after a minute, his voice compressed fury. "And so we will give it to you." His upper lip curls as he pauses and I can feel his eyes boring into me, to the others, through his shades.

Bile gathers at the back of my throat.

"It's simple," he says, his voice a blade of steel. "You have until midnight to tell us where she is. If we don't have her by then, someone in this room will be shot."

CHAPTER 10

Ariel

"Do you want water?" Milo asks. Usually I keep a glass on the shelf over my bathroom sink but it got smashed when my room was ransacked.

"No," I say. I clear my throat, which is still tender. "Milo, thanks for coming and holding my hair and stuff." I'm feeling more together and can now appreciate not having hair covered in puke.

But Milo frowns. "My name isn't Milo."

Oh.

"It's Nico." He looks at me, his brow furrowed. "I've worked for you for three years and you don't even know my name?"

I try to shrug it off. "I was close."

"Really?" he asks and for the first time his voice isn't ringing with honesty and goodness. It's ringing with sarcasm.

I suck in a breath. I hate to eat crow but I know it's not optional. "I'm sorry," I say, looking at him instead of looking at the floor, which I'd prefer.

"People matter and their names matter," he says with deep conviction.

I let out a long impatient breath. But he is my only ally and I can't have him angry at me. "Yes, people matter and their names matter," I say through gritted teeth. "Nico is a wonderful name."

"It means victory of the people."

I snort, then see he's looking wounded again. "Oh, that's really cool." I don't sound that sincere but he lets it pass.

"Yeah, it definitely inspires me," he says. "My mom said she chose it because the first time she held me she knew she wanted more for me, not just a life farming or slaving away making minimum wage, but doing something meaningful that helped people." His smile is tinged with sadness that somehow has me talking before I think.

"My mom named me Ariel because it means lioness of God," I say. "She wanted me to be strong."

My mom was weak, both physically and mentally, and I think she hoped I'd manage the world a little better than she did in her short life.

"That's really powerful," Nico says solemnly.

Why am I telling him stuff like this? I never even think about my mom, let alone talk about her. "It's not like it means anything. I mean, here you are working a minimum wage job and helping hold a group of high school students hostage so someone can get rich off my dad's company. Not exactly a victory for the people."

His whole body seems to fold in. "I didn't have a choice."

"You said that before." I am finally feeling well enough to stand up, though my stomach feels lined with acid.

"The people trying to get money from your dad's company found out about us before they came and tried to recruit us to help," he says, leaning back against the pink bathroom wall. He looks out of place in his fatigues. "Most people agreed to help for the money. But those of us who refused at first—they had other incentives for us."

I don't think I want to know anymore.

"My dad is here illegally," he says. "He works for a family in Greenwich and if he gets reported to immigration, he'll be deported. I could go home to El Salvador but he can't. He was too outspoken in his politics and he made enemies in the government. If he goes home he will be killed."

He says it simply but the hollowness in his voice tells me how much he has thought about this, how trapped he feels.

"I had no choice but to agree," he says. "But I figured I'd do what my dad did back home and work from the inside to see if I could make a difference."

"So helping me is a difference?" I thought his motive was a crush on me but a political motive is even better—more conviction. I take a moment to drink some water, my hands cupped under the faucet. It tastes divine.

"It's a starting point," he says. "What they're doing is wrong and I want to help stop it."

"Great," I say.

"So you will help?"

I raise an eyebrow. "Obviously." Anything that stops this early will help Abby. In fact I realize now is the time to tell him about Abby.

He shakes his head before I can speak. "I don't mean just to save yourself. I mean, will you help to stop this, to save everyone if you can, even if it means making sacrifices?"

"Yes." I'm surprised that it stings to learn that he thinks I'm a spoiled brat who would leave everyone to die if she could save her own skin doing it, but whatever. I'm not telling him about Abby.

"There are a few of us on the inside," he says, suddenly sounding professional. "I think it's better if you don't know who they are. But we can help."

"Can you get a phone?" I ask. That would be the easiest and quickest way to end this.

But Nico shakes his head. "All phones are locked away in the office. None of us has access."

"That sucks," I say, thinking how much a phone could have helped.

"But there are still things we can do. And we need to see which of the hostages will help."

"That makes sense."

"Who do you trust?" he asks simply.

"Sera."

Wait, did I really just say the name of the biggest backstabber of all time? But as I think about it, I realize it's true. I know everyone downstairs pretty well. And there's only one person I am certain would do everything she could to stop anyone else from being hurt.

"I'm not sure we can stop the killing at midnight," Nico says, running a hand through his short black hair. "But—"

"Wait, what killing?"

His eyes are filled with sadness. "I wasn't thinking," he says softly. "You wouldn't know. They are looking for you, the agents."

I nod, suddenly feel the acid again, burning into my stomach lining.

"They have threatened your classmates. If you are not found by midnight, one of them will be shot."

Somehow he knows what this information will do to me because his arms are reaching for me before my legs even give out. He lowers me slowly, gently to the floor. Maybe he doesn't just think I'm a spoiled brat.

I look at the clock. It's 11:03. Less than an hour until someone dies.

I lean my head back and close my eyes. How can I keep hiding?

"I need to turn myself in," I say. I feel the wave gathering power at my feet, ready to sweep me off. "I can't let someone die because of me."

"You can't turn yourself in," he says.

"Why not?" I ask, turning to look at him. His eyes are light brown, like honey in the sun. "How can I put my life over theirs, say my life matters more, that I deserve to live while one of them dies?"

The words burst out of me because in my heart I don't believe I do. There are some pretty good people down there, people who want to be like Nico, make the world better and stuff. Ella wants to be a doctor and work for Doctors Without Borders—she even interned in their New York office this summer. Mike wants to be a diplomat and Cassidy wants to be an attorney who prosecutes people who hurt children, something she will be amazing at. And what goals do I have? Not any really.

"That's not what it's about," Nico says. His features are broad, his eyes deep set and his face round. I thought he was plain-looking but in this moment I see a beauty in his face. "You're a distraction for the agents. That's what we need, distractions. Because that's when things slip by them and they make mistakes. Those moments are our only real opportunities to do something."

"So I need to stay alive to be a distraction?" I ask.

He smiles and his face shines. "You're a lot more than that, but yes, for now we need you to be a distraction."

He reaches over and smoothes a lock of hair out of my face. It's a moment when another guy would lean in and kiss me but I can see now that that is not Nico's intention, in fact I don't think it ever would be. He doesn't have a crush on me at all. He just likes me as a person. And that has me feeling weak in the knees the way a crush never does. Because it means he doesn't see me as something he can own or use. He just sees me, Ariel.

"Abby's coming here tomorrow," I blurt out.

His face falls, he totally gets it. "What time?"

"Noon."

He nods, thinking. "Then we have to get this taken care of before noon."

I could hug him, though obviously I won't. "That would be great," I say instead.

He smiles. "Abby has a real green thumb."

I suddenly remember that sometimes my little sister hangs out in the garden with Nico "helping" him plant things. I never thought a lot about it but it is awfully nice of him to let her play when he is trying to get work done.

We hear footsteps in the hall and we both scramble to our feet.

"Quickly," he breathes, and I sprint to the fireplace.

Once I am in he sets the grate behind me. "I will go to Sera," he whispers. "To see if she will help."

And then he is gone.

CHAPTER 11

Sera

After The Assassin stalks out a few people start crying. Ella appears on the verge of collapse and Mike is hugging her, patting her back. A couple of agents stand in the doorway of the hall that leads to the kitchen and two sit on the sofas, guns casually resting on their laps.

I look at the clock above the fireplace. It's 11:03. We have fifty-seven minutes before—I put my head down on my knees, unable to complete the thought.

"Are you okay?" Hudson asks, and I feel his hand rest gently on my back. "I mean, obviously not but you know what I mean."

He thinks I am upset about the fact that one of us will die at midnight. Which I am, of course. But it's so much more. I know where Ariel is. If they haven't found her yet there's only one place she could be and that's the tunnels. But how could I tell them that? Yet if I don't, someone, possibly me, will be shot. I feel like my head is going to split open.

"What's going on?" he asks.

I don't want to tell him. It's enough that I've burdened him with the phone when I barely even know the guy. Though on the other hand, I'm not sure I can handle it alone. I sit up, as always careful to keep my arm with the phone turned in.

"You're scaring me." Hudson is looking at my face closely and he rests his hands on top of mine. For whatever it's worth, in this moment he really does know me.

I take a deep breath and glance around to make sure no agents are nearby. "I know where Ariel is."

Hudson gives out a low whistle and sits back. "Okay," he says slowly. "That's a lot of information to have."

"Too much. I feel like I have to choose between Ariel or one of the hostages, maybe even me, and I just can't decide because—"

Hudson pats my hand softly and I realize I am talking a mile a minute and my face is heating up.

I take another deep breath. "If I tell them where she is, who knows what they'll do to her," I say it a bit more calmly, but then I am shocked when tears prick my eyes. "But if I say nothing, I've killed someone else."

"Not true. You're not killing anyone. The people with the guns are doing that."

"I know, but—"

He raises a hand to cut me off. "I know what you mean. But you can't think about it like that because it's not what's actually happening. They're going to kill someone at midnight and you have no say in that. All you have is some information, nothing more. All the choices are theirs. They might say they'd only take Ariel, or only shoot one of us, but they have all the power. They can kill anyone at anytime and whatever you say or don't say won't change that."

He's right and thinking about it this way is both better and worse. But the question is still there. "So do I tell them or not?"

I want him to make this choice for me, to take it out of my hands, though I know him well enough now to know he won't.

"What do you think?" he asks.

I take a moment to picture what would happen if I tell them where Ariel is. Agents would crawl into the tunnels, the walls would echo with their footsteps as they hunted Ariel. She would hear them, try to run, to hide, but there would be no escape. She would be trapped and they would find her. And then what would they do with her, now that her dad, the only one who could get the company money—at least as far as I know—is dead? I don't want to know the answer to that question.

Ariel was the one who stayed up with me all night long the night I was seven and our cat Snickerdoodle got killed by a neighbor's dog. She called me twenty times a day during the two-week period when my mom left my dad, and then called me every Tuesday for six months after so I could make fun of all the stuff that happened in our family therapy sessions. Yeah, she hates me and has made me miserable for the past nine months and four days. But I can't do this to her. I just can't.

"I'm not turning her in." There is space in my chest as I say the words, an opening. I made the right choice. And then I realize something else. "But I can't just sit around waiting for them to execute someone. Or just playing with this stupid phone all night, hoping I get lucky with it."

Hudson nods. "We need to do a little brush-busting."

"What?"

"It's a hunting term for when the animal sees you and ruins your shot before you can take it."

I wrinkle my nose. "You hunt? That's so mean."

He gives me a withering stare. "We hunt for meat. And we use a lot more of the animal than you do when you pick up a steak at the grocery store."

I think about it for a moment. "Okay, you've shamed me with my meat from the supermarket," I say. "I'm with you. Let's do a little brush-busting."

He laughs. "It sounds really funny when you say it." The look in his eyes makes my pulse dance for the tiniest second.

"So what do we do?" I ask, getting down to business.

That look doesn't mean anything. This is a guy who dates lingerie models and movie stars. He is not flirting with a flat-chested high school kid whose most interesting life experience involved painting sets for the high school play. And there are way more important things to be thinking about.

Hudson runs a hand through his hair, making it stick up in that way I like. I look away.

"I don't know," he says. He looks around to make sure no agents have come near us but they are still just in the doorways, keeping watch but too far away to hear what we're saying. "I guess that's the million-dollar question. And we don't have much time to figure it out. Is there some way we could use the tunnels?"

"I don't know," I say. "I mean, I guess if there was something we could get from another section of the house to help us, but I can't think of anything except computers and without Internet . . ."

"No gun collection, huh?" he asks in a voice that indicates he knows the answer.

I roll my eyes. "Plus the house is crawling with agents looking for Ariel. If—"

I stop suddenly. An agent is coming toward us. The phone. I press my arm into my stomach so that no trace of the phone shows. My heart is thumping hard in my chest and I reach for Hudson's hand without even thinking. He grabs my fingers tight and moves so he is sitting up straight. I sit up too, gulping shallow breaths.

The agent stops right in front of us, sits on the sofa with his back to the room, then slowly lifts his ski mask. For a second I'm just confused and then I realize I know him.

"Nico?" I ask in disbelief.

"Ssh," he says, quickly pulling the mask back over his face. "I need you to get a plate of food and bring it to the east staircase in exactly ten minutes," he says quietly. Then he stands up.

"I don't understand," I say. If he wants food he can just get it.

"You will," he says, and then he walks away, leaving us both staring after him.

CHAPTER 12

Ariel

I change quickly and stuff my party clothes in the tunnel. I don't need anyone finding them. It feels good to be in dark jeans and an old black sweater and it's a lot more practical for navigating the dusty tunnels. I pull my hair back in a ponytail that probably looks like hell but who cares. Then I start down the narrow hall of the tunnel to see what's going on near my dad's office suite.

I sit for a few minutes, my back pressed against the cool plaster wall, but there's nothing except the scent of a fire wafting in the air. Which pisses me off—I can't believe they set a fire in the huge freestanding fireplace in my dad's office to make their work environment nicer while they steal my dad's company.

The smell reminds me of something I haven't thought about in years. Once when we were nine Sera and I planned a campout in my backyard, complete with a fire in the fire pit where we'd roast organic hot dogs and make s'mores. But at the last minute it rained so John said we could do it in my dad's office. We spread out our sleeping bags on the cream-colored rug and laid a tarp down to eat on. We stuffed ourselves, then snuggled into our sleeping bags and talked about what we wanted to do when we grew up as the fire burned down, the flames going lower and lower. They were typical nine-year-old dreams, like having an apartment together in New York City, being Broadway stars, marrying brothers so we'd be sisters. But it felt so real that night, like we'd really be able to do all of it.

And look at us now. I smile bitterly in the dark. What is Sera going to say when Nico approaches her? Is it going to be the thing that pushes her to turn me in? Or will she just laugh in his face? That's not her style; she'd just politely say no thanks. And I don't want to think about how that will make me feel. Or how I'll feel if it goes the other way and I actually have to talk to her for the first time in nine months and four days.

I can't sit still anymore, with memories haunting me and the minutes ticking down, so I head toward the back wing of the house, where my dad's bedroom is. Maybe there's something there worth finding. He does have a safe after all.

When I get to the grate in his room I flip open the latch, walk quietly in, and then stop short. His room has been even more destroyed than mine. His $5,000 suits are a heap of sliced-up cashmere and silk on the floor, the new one he bought for his lawyer's funeral on top of the pile. His bed has been destroyed down to the box spring and it's wet. A smell is coming from it, something acidic and sour. Did someone pee on his bed? That would be beyond vile and I breathe through my mouth so I don't have to think about it.

I wait for a moment, listening, then creep silently out into the room, my feet crunching on broken glass from the pictures he had up on the mantel. I take the one of him and my mom on their wedding day and the one of him holding me when I was a newborn. My mom is the one who framed it but my dad looks really happy in it, smiling down at baby me. He doesn't look like a guy who will end up going on month-long business trips six times a year, leaving his child with his assistant and a housekeeper. But pictures, like so many things, lie.

The thing is, even knowing this, I can't look at the picture or any of his things too long. If I do, I feel movement deep in my gut, that primal grief straining to break free, to pour out in one long, endless wail. Which is not going to happen, not when I have Abby to consider.

I put both photos in the tunnel, then make my way to his safe. It's on the side wall, behind a landscape my mom painted. That would be nice except my dad said the safe needed to have a painting covering it that wasn't at all valuable because it would be touched. I remember how my mom's face fell when he said it.

I'm not sure if there will be anything useful in the safe. It's not like he kept a gun there because we had armed guards around the clock and an incredible security system. Plus my dad just wasn't a gun guy. But maybe I'll find some papers, something that will tell me who is behind this. The more time I have to sit and stew, the more I want to know who's doing this.

I flip open the painting and punch in the code, the one my dad uses as his password for everything: Swann161. It's for his favorite football player, Lynn Swann, and the 161 receiving yards he caught in Super Bowl X. This is the kind of thing you know if your dad is a rabid Steelers fan. *Was*.

The safe opens with a soft click. Empty. Someone got here before me, someone else who knows my dad well enough to know his code. Or maybe he emptied it himself?

I go over to his nightstand. The top has been swept clear, the lamp that used to be on it lies smashed on the wall. But inside the drawer there's a business magazine and under that a printout of something. I pick it up and realize it's the plan for my party, this night that has gone so horribly wrong. The first page has a list of scheduled events and the page underneath has details of who is taking care of what.

I start to read it more closely but then I hear movement in the hall and leap through the open grate, pulling it quickly closed behind me. I head for my room, putting the plan in my pocket. I should really just get rid of it since there's nothing useful on it, but somehow I want to hold onto it a bit longer. I walk as quickly and quietly as I can. Nico will have told Sera by now and I need to get back. It's not really a big deal if she refuses to help. How much help will she be, really?

But somehow I can't seem to fully convince myself of this as I slip quietly through the tunnels, my heart in my throat.

CHAPTER 13

Sera

"That was so weird," I say as Nico walks away. My heart is settling back down but I'm still confused. What does he mean, I will understand?

"Yeah," Hudson says. "Nothing about that made sense. And who's Nico?"

"He's the gardener here," I say. "Or one of them anyway. He's one of those people who always seems happy to be doing exactly what he's doing. And he grows beautiful plants." I think of the incredible hydrangeas they had two summers ago that were his pride and joy.

"So when he's not participating in a hostage scheme he grows flowers," Hudson says dryly.

"I'm surprised he's part of this."

It doesn't fit with how I always thought of Nico. Though I guess you could argue I barely knew him. He could be a serial killer and I'd be the last person to know. Still, he always seemed genuinely nice.

"A lot of surprises tonight," Hudson says. He glances out the window where we can see shadowed forms roaming about.

"Yeah, that's for sure." I rub my eyes. I'm usually asleep by now. "I guess I need to prepare a plate of food, whatever that means. Will you hold the phone while I go?"

Hudson shakes his head. "I'm going with you."

"I think I can get food on a plate without help," I say. "And someone has to hold the phone."

"I mean I'm going with you to meet that guy. We'll put the phone back in the sofa while we're gone."

"No. We can't risk losing it or someone finding it. And he didn't ask for you, just me."

"I'm coming," he says, and in that moment I hear just the tiniest Southern drawl in his voice. "And I don't think we can risk having the phone on us. I doubt we'll be gone that long anyway."

He's probably right. I tuck my hand in between the cushions and shimmy the phone out. But I still don't want him to try to come with me, it's too dangerous.

"We'd better hurry," he says, standing up. "You have less than seven minutes to prepare that plate and it's like a five-minute walk just to get to the kitchen."

"I don't want you to get hurt," I say quietly as we walk through the living room.

Hudson turns so suddenly I almost run into him.

"Do you honestly think I'm just going to watch you go off with that guy who could do pretty much anything he wanted?" he asks sharply, then glances around quickly to make sure he wasn't overheard.

I can see in his face that his mind is going bad places, and though I can't imagine Nico being a rapist, I'm guessing some of the other agents could be. What if they sent him to get the nearest available girl? The Assassin said no one would get hurt but he hasn't exactly inspired trust.

"Yeah, that'd be great if you'd come," I say quietly.

He nods, then turns and heads to the doorway where we ask the agent standing there for permission to enter the kitchen. He grants it and in we go. I grab a plate and we pile on hors d'oeuvre, then practically run to the doorway facing the hall.

It's been exactly ten minutes. A guard is disappearing upstairs and moments later another one appears. He pauses when he sees us, then hurries down.

"I meant you alone," Nico whispers.

"I go where she goes," Hudson says.

The drawl is there and his stance is no longer slouchy rock star. He stands tall, his chest wide, and I can see the boy who went hunting and took down a buffalo or whatever they hunt in Appalachia. Whatever it was didn't stand a chance against this guy.

"You can't," Nico whispers, looking around almost frantically.

Hudson stands firm and silent, staring at Nico.

Nico lets out a frustrated breath. "Okay."

He glances at the agent in the far doorway who is slouched over, not even really looking at us. I guess they're getting tired too. We go out the door but instead of going back to the living room Nico rushes up the stairs. Hudson and I exchange a look, then we hurry after him, Hudson holding tight to my hand, my other hand holding the plate.

Nico walks quickly down the hall, his steps light. Without even thinking about it I realize I am practically tiptoeing as well. Why the secrecy?

He passes the first guest suite and the upstairs game room, then turns down a hall that is a little too familiar, with the red-and-blue Oriental carpet Ariel and I once spilled hot cocoa on—I bet the stains are still there, though Ariel's dad never found them— and the series of Art Wolfe photos along the walls. There's one of a leopard that I love but I don't look at it as we go by.

I hope more than anything that we will pass the doorway on the left, the one that leads to Ariel's suite, but this is where Nico stops. He turns to quickly usher us inside, taking the plate from me as I step around him. Hudson goes first, his hand wrapped firmly around mine.

The light is off but Nico comes in after us, closes the door softly, and then turns on the light. I see we are not alone. Someone is standing in front of the fireplace and when she turns to face us it's all I can do not to scream.

It's Ariel.

CHAPTER 14

Ariel

"Don't scream," I say quickly. I can tell she's about to.

Sera presses her lips tight together and her look of surprise turns into a glare. "I can't believe this," she says.

Actually talking to Sera after all this time is making my chest all fluttery, like a bunch of feathers are blowing around in there. I'm not sure what to say and it all feels harder with the stupid rock star she dragged along. I take a moment to give Nico a look.

"What's he doing here?"

Nico has taken off the ridiculous ski mask, and he shrugs as he sits down in my desk chair and sets the plate of food on a clear spot on my desk. My emptied out stomach growls but now is not the time to eat.

"He insisted," Nico says. "Sera remembered my name by the way."

I roll my eyes, shoving away the stab of guilt I feel when I see how much this meant to him.

"You didn't remember his name?" Sera asks in that self-righteous way she has when she is being nice and I am not.

"Wait, I thought he worked for your family," Hudson says in his Southern drawl that sounds fake, kind of like his stupid phony music.

I throw up my hands. "Really? We're going to worry about me forgetting his name and not the guys with guns who've taken over my house?"

"People's names do matter," Sera says, not willing to just let it go.

I glance at Nico and am irritated to see he is grinning.

"Okay, I'm a horrible person who doesn't respect the people who work in my home," I say. "Forgetting his name was unforgivable."

Sera smiles. "Just as long as you admit it."

I feel a tugging in my chest, a feeling I've had a lot over these past nine months and four days, a feeling I've done all I can do to stamp out. Because I hate Sera and missing her is weak.

"Can we focus please?" I ask.

But now Sera is looking around the room, her eyes darkening as she takes in the damage. "They did this?" she asks.

I can almost see her remembering sleepovers under the goose down comforter whose feathers now cover the bed like snow. And knowing which pictures go in which frames even though they are now bent and mixed in with crushed glass.

"It's just stuff," I say, looking away from her. I can't think about what any of the things on the floor mean to me, not right now. "We have more important things to worry about."

Nico straightens up. "Yeah, we don't have much time."

"Time for what exactly?" Hudson asks.

He walks carefully around the glass to sit on the sofa, which has a few gouges in it but is still functional, and Sera follows. I stay standing next to the fireplace in case I need to make a quick escape.

"Settle down rock star, you aren't even supposed to be here," I snap. Somehow everything feels harder with him here.

But Nico gives me a look that says I'm being a moron. "The more people the better," he says.

"The more people for what?" Sera asks. Her chocolate brown curls are starting to leak out of the twist she pulled them, the way they always do.

"We want to plan an escape, to get everyone out before anyone else gets hurt," Nico answers.

"Says the man helping to hold us hostage," Hudson says in that stupid Southern drawl.

"He's working undercover," I say sharply. "He was blackmailed into helping them and he's doing everything he can to figure out a plan to stop this."

Nico's eyes light up at my defense of his being there and for a moment there is a spark in the air between us. I look away fast.

Sera nods. "That makes sense."

Apparently Sera's seal of approval is all it takes for the rock star. "So what's the plan?" he asks. "Because I am done sitting around and waiting to be offed by one of these guys."

"That's why we wanted to meet with you," Nico says. "Ariel said Sera was the person she trusted most so we figured we'd start by talking with her to try to come up with something."

Sera's whole body stiffens at his words. "Is that so?" she says, turning to me, her eyes narrowed. "I'm the one you trust?"

I forgot how cutting Sera's sarcasm is.

"I know you and I have a lot to talk about," I say, just because I have to say something. I don't actually want to talk about anything except a plan to end this hostage situation.

"Do you really think a talk is going to make up for what you did to me?" she asks, her face turning a blotchy red.

"What I did to *you*?" I ask, feeling my own face heat up.

"We can't do this now." Hudson's voice is soft and I can tell from the way he glances at Sera that she has told him the story and he has taken her side. But when he looks at me I don't see judgment. "It's getting closer to midnight and we're better off working together to try and figure out a plan."

I know he's right but it takes a supreme effort to bite back what I want to say to Sera.

"We'll table it," Sera says, already calmed down but giving me a hard look before continuing. "And I think we have what we need. I got your dad's cell phone."

I am electrified by her words. "Where is it? Why haven't you called 911 already?"

"It's password protected," Hudson says. "We couldn't figure out the password."

"Give it to me," I say, reaching out my hand. I can't believe that in less than a minute I'll be on the phone with the police and this whole nightmare will be in the past, long before Abby ever gets here.

But Sera and the rock star exchange a look.

"We don't have it on us," he says.

I press my lips together so I don't scream in frustration. "Where is it?" I ask as calmly as I can.

"We left it in the sofa," Sera says. "But no one will look for it there."

Nico proves yet again how well he knows me by placing a hand on the small of my back so that I don't explode at Sera and Hudson.

"They were smart to leave it," he says gently. "They didn't know where I was taking them."

I take a deep breath and even though I am still furious that the answer is so close, yet so far, I know he's right. "So how fast can you get it to me? Or should I just tell you the code and you use it?"

"I don't think we can use it now," Hudson says reluctantly. "We're being watched too closely. But Sera can sneak it back in her sleeve and if you can get us back up here," he nods at Nico, "we can give it to you."

Nico's brow creases. "I don't think I can get you back up here for another half-hour, when the guards change and there's that few minutes when no one's at that staircase."

"A half-hour is too long," Hudson says. "It'll be after midnight. Can we just give it to you down there?"

Nico shakes his head. "I can't walk back into the living room again without someone asking me why. And if I keep going back downstairs someone will notice. The best I can do is be back in half an hour and even that is pushing it."

"Okay, then we'll have to figure out a way to buy some extra time," Hudson says. "Some kind of false lead to send them on so they postpone killing anyone while they search."

Sera jumps up, excited. "The basement in the garage," she says a bit too loudly.

Nico raises a finger to his lips.

"That's really hard to find if you don't know about it," she says more softly as the rest of us look at her blankly. "I'll say that's where I think Ariel's hiding. By the time they get out there and check, we'll have had enough time to get you the phone."

"Perfect," Hudson says, his eyes shining like Sera's some kind of genius.

Though I have to admit it's a pretty good idea. It will take them a while to figure out which floorboards to move to get into the hidden space beneath the floor. And then something else occurs to me. I step into the tunnel and then return with one of my silver satin pumps, the ones I was wearing with my party dress. I hand it to Nico.

"What if you planted this outside, between the garage and the house? That would make it look even more plausible that I was somewhere outside."

"Great idea," Sera says. "The more evidence the better."

Nico takes the shoe. "I think the best I can do is toss it out a window and hope no one sees it fall."

"Do it out the window of the back guest bedroom," I say. "That area isn't well lit by the floodlights but you'd probably see it if you were walking from the back door to the garage. Just, you know, make sure no one's there before you throw it."

Nico gives me a surprisingly withering look. "Yeah, I think I know to avoid hitting someone with your shoe when we're trying to make it look like you lost it running to the garage."

He's funny when he tries to be sarcastic. And kind of cute too, a thought I quickly squelch.

"So we have a plan," Hudson says.

Voices come from the hall and we all freeze. Then I leap into the fireplace. I wait for Nico to set the grate in place but there is a pause and then he passes me the food from the plate Sera brought up, that he's put on a shoe box top. I can't believe he thought of me being hungry when we're under pressure like this.

I take it from his hands, then listen as he leaves with Sera and Hudson. I wait until their steps, muffled by the carpet, fade, and then I dig into the food. The cold shrimp rolls are tough and doughy, the bacon and goat cheese rolls hard with grease. But I am too hungry to care, stuffing every last morsel into my mouth. Then I stand up and head for the living room, hoping against hope that our plan will work and that no one will die at midnight.

CHAPTER 15

Sera

Nico peeks out before hustling us into the main hall and then down the stairs. This time my heart is in my throat for another reason: I don't want Nico to have to explain why he has taken us out of the specified area—the empty plate is really a flimsy reason for two people to have gone upstairs.

Fortunately, we make it to the kitchen without being seen.

Nico, who is back in his ski mask, says, "I'll come get you in thirty minutes." He says it so softly it's more like breath than words. He nods at the agent in the kitchen, then heads back upstairs.

"How are you doing?" Hudson asks quietly, eyeing the agent standing in the other doorway.

Another agent joins the one in the kitchen and they start talking in low voices. I sag back against the wall, letting it hold me up. I can't believe we just saw Ariel, that this was our first conversation in nine months and four days. I think it's the first time we've even had eye contact since she got back from the facility.

"Overwhelmed," I say finally.

"She's intense," Hudson says, getting a glass of water.

"Yeah," I say, the word coming out as a sigh. "That can be awesome when you're party planning or doing a school project. But not so much when she's working to make your life hell."

He gulps down half the glass, then passes it to me. I take a sip, feeling coolness trickle down my throat. It gives me the strength to move over to one of the bar stools. The hors d'oeuvre are still on the counter, grease congealed in lumps around the food.

"She misses you, you know."

I laugh, something I wouldn't have guessed was possible as the minutes tick down to midnight. "Right."

"Seriously," he says.

He's obviously just trying to be nice because if there's one thing I'm certain of it's that Ariel does not miss me. That she has made abundantly clear.

"We need to get the phone," I whisper. We've been speaking too quietly for the agents in the doorway to overhear but I'm not taking chances.

"Just one second." Hudson opens the fridge.

"I can't believe you're still hungry."

"My mama used to say that I could eat a whole turkey and be back at the kitchen asking for a snack an hour later," he says, taking out an apple.

I smile, as much at the fact that he calls his mother "mama" as the story itself. And I love the Southern drawl that has been creeping into his voice this past hour.

"Let's go," he says.

Everyone is pretty much still sitting where they were when we left. I guess we weren't gone that long but so much has happened. Then I see something that makes me stop in my tracks. An agent is sitting on our sofa. Panic pierces me at the thought of the phone slithering out from its hiding place and falling on the floor, or even just poking up above the edge of the cushion, but when I can bear to look, there is no sign of it.

"What are we going to do?" I hiss. We have to get that phone.

"I don't know," he says, biting his lip.

We are by the poker table and he sets the apple down, his appetite obviously killed. I want to say something, to come up with some kind of plan, but then I see my classmates standing up and heading toward the chairs where The Assassin told us to sit at midnight. And now my stomach lurches for a whole other awful reason.

"We should probably go sit," Hudson says. "You ready?"

"No," I say, trying to make it sound like a joke but failing.

He takes my hand. "Me neither."

Groups of girls sit close, the guys are in clusters hovering nearby. No one is really talking. I guess there isn't a lot to say. Cassidy looks like she accidently bit a lemon when she notices me and Hudson but other than that no one bothers with us as we sit down.

All the seats in the back are taken, of course, so we end up in the front row of chairs, next to the other people deemed most expendable by the class. I'm surprised to see Ella there but less surprised to see Noah and Lulu, two grinds who don't really do anything social. I notice Franz toward the back, his nose swollen, his shirt stained with blood.

The grandfather clock in the corner begins to strike midnight and a taut silence falls over the group. The air feels heavy, like it does right before a shattering thunderstorm.

At the eleventh chime The Assassin walks in. The rest of the agents look alike but there is something to his walk that lets you know exactly who he is. He strides over to our group and easily grabs Mike from the back row where he is sitting next to Cassidy. People near them lean out of the way as fast as they can, like Mike is now contagious.

The Assassin walks Mike to the front of the chairs, places the gun at his temple, and then turns to us.

"So who has some information for me?" he asks in his calm voice.

Mike's eyes are shut tight but tears begin to leak out, making his face shine in the harsh light. An hour ago he was making jokes in the kitchen and now he is terrified for his life.

My chest is so tight I can feel my heart working to beat in the small space it has left and my lungs are having trouble filling. I think I might faint. But Hudson squeezes my hand and I somehow manage to make it to my feet.

"Um, I thought of another place Ariel might be," I say. My voice sounds like it belongs to a stranger but I press on. "It's in the garage, it's this bomb shelter under the floor."

"Okay," The Assassin says.

Relief floods through me so fast I lose the ability to stand and sit back hard on the metal chair. Hudson squeezes my hand and I turn to him, relief making my body feel light. We got the time! And then I hear the gunshot.

CHAPTER 16

Ariel

One minute Mike is a person and the next minute he is an open wound, his head a leaking mess of red and gray and gore, his body falling, lifeless, on the floor. I press my hands against my mouth, holding in my scream. It slips out the sides but there is so much screaming in the living room that mine goes unheard.

I close my eyes but the image is seared in my brain, calling up the matching images of Bianca and my father. It takes everything in me but I push them away, into the dark place in my mind, and shut the door. My face is wet with tears and sweat but I crawl back to the grate and look out into the living room.

Agents are cleaning up the mess that was Mike—that I don't look at. Pretty much everyone is having some kind of breakdown, crying, wailing, sobbing in someone else's arms. Cassidy's face is sharply etched but I see tears on her face. Ella has collapsed in Lulu's lap and there is blood on her hair that Lulu is not touching. Sera is next to her and I'm surprised to see that she's not having a meltdown. Sera melts down over mice in traps so this should put her over the edge. But it hasn't. Her face is ashen and she's holding Hudson's hands so tightly I can see her skin turn white around the knuckles. But there are no tears, no cries, just a deep pain in her eyes. I can't help but wonder if she's keeping it together or if she's fallen into some kind of catatonic state.

The Assassin is still standing in front of everyone, gun in hand. He is waiting for people to be quiet. Slowly, when people realize he is still there, the cries soften to low moans and people sit up. After a minute it's so quiet I hear fabric rustle when Ella sits up. No one wants to give The Assassin a reason to shoot anyone else.

The sweat on my face and body has dried and now I feel chilled sitting here alone on the hard floor. I wrap my arms around myself and wait for The Assassin to speak.

"Your friend was not here at midnight so someone was shot, as promised," The Assassin says in his neutral tone. He looks at Sera. "If we find her in the garage, then you can all relax. But if not, I'd advise you to do some careful thinking about why you would protect the person who just let your friend die. And I promise you, if she is not found soon, he will not be the only one to die tonight."

His words slice into me so deeply I almost cry out. This is my fault. Mike would be alive if I hadn't hidden and stayed hidden. Or if I hadn't changed seats with Bianca. But he lost his life so that I can keep mine and I'm not sure I can live with how worthless that makes me feel.

"We'll let you know what we find," The Assassin says, and then he is gone.

I feel such hatred for him it scorches my insides. But it's nothing compared to the hatred I feel for myself. I can't do this, I can't stay hidden any longer. I see Nico's point about my disappearance as a distraction, but it's not worth more lives. *I'm* not worth more lives.

Last weekend we all went to the movies and Mike bought this big tub of popcorn. I'm not sure what started it but halfway through the movie all the guys started throwing popcorn at each other, the girls screaming and ducking to avoid getting that gross butter stuff on our faces and clothes. The manager came and threw us all out. On the way out of the aisle I grabbed the tub with the last bits of popcorn and seeds at the bottom, and once we were in the parking lot I dumped it on Mike's head. Some guys would get all bent out of shape about a girl getting the final shot but Mike just laughed and told me we'd make a great Bonnie and Clyde if I'd ever agree to go out with him.

And now he's dead at eighteen.

I can't do this for a second longer. I am up, running through the tunnels to find Nico, to figure out the best way to turn myself in to The Assassin so that we can be sure no one else gets hurt. Maybe Nico can set up some sort of bargain, buy some kind of favor to help with his plan. I'll tell him the code so Sera can call for help but I'm not doing this for a single second longer.

I slip on some dust on the top stair and fall to my knees, which is surprisingly painful. My palms sting too from landing on them. I take a moment to rub them together and check to see if I scraped my knees. They seem fine though, just bruised, but it's enough to make me stop and think. Abby. If I turn myself in, what will happen to Abby?

Before I can answer my own question I hear voices in the hall. Several guys are talking and one of the voices is familiar.

I creep quietly to the nearest grate and see two agents walking down the hall, my uncle between them. My breath catches when I see his wild red hair, stripped of his Yankees hat and looking like he just walked through a hurricane, which I guess in some ways he has.

"Next step," an agent is saying. He is probably one of the higher-ups and I desperately wish I could see behind his disguise, to know who plotted this.

"We've set everything up for the transfer of funds," a second agent says.

They are walking right past the grate and I catch a whiff of Uncle Marc's overpowering Hermes cologne, the kind my dad buys him every year and then complains about when Uncle Marc pats on like half the bottle every time he comes over.

"So I just need to sign the rest of the documents?" Uncle Marc asks.

My stomach drops.

"Yes," the first agent says. "Then you'll have the funds at your fingertips."

"Ready to deposit in the Swiss account," the second agent adds.

Uncle Marc nods and replies but they are too far away to hear, that or the ringing in my ears from his words is too loud.

I slip down to the floor, the wall of the tunnel holding me up as my mind takes baby steps toward understanding this, hoping against hope that I am somehow figuring it wrong. But there doesn't seem to be any room for misinterpretation, a fact that has me shivering from the cold, ugly truth. The person behind the hostage situation, the shooting of my father and friends, and this night of terror is not some stranger.

It is my very own uncle.

CHAPTER 17

Sera

The room is chaos after The Assassin stalks out. Two other agents are cleaning up the soggy pile on the floor that was once Mike's brain while his body is being carried out by another, and most of my classmates are crying. But my eyes are dry and I'm not shaking or moaning or having flashback images fly through my mind. I didn't know it until right this second, but something in me froze over when Mr. Barett and Bianca were killed, their empty bodies on this same floor. Seeing Mike does not shred me apart, not like that. It sits in my stomach, corrosive and nauseating, but it doesn't threaten to engulf me, not like the first deaths did.

Hudson is looking at me, I think waiting for my delayed meltdown.

"This is not okay," I tell him.

He looks slightly alarmed, like I might be on the verge of losing it, but this time I'm not.

"None of this is okay," I continue, sweeping out my arm and banging my wrist on the chair in back of me. It hurts but I don't really care. "They shot Mike like he was nothing, like he wasn't someone's kid and . . . " Here come the tears. They slide down my face but slowly, not out of control, and I can still talk. "They just destroyed his parents' and his brother's lives without even thinking about it."

Hudson nods, still looking at me like I might collapse.

"And they will do it again," I say, with a sniff because now my nose is running. "And we just, we can't let them do it again." The words make more tears come, but I'm still not falling apart.

"Okay," Hudson says.

I realize there are tears in his eyes too and for a moment the absurdity of it hits me, that we're here, being held, watching people die. "Is it weird that I still can't believe this is actually happening?"

He grins for a second, though the tears are still there. "Probably, but that's exactly how I feel too," he says. "Like I just have these moments when I think I must be dreaming or something."

"Yeah," I say, leaning back with a sigh. The tears are slowing. Without thinking I turn my hand and lace my fingers with Hudson's. When I realize what I've done, I want to take it back— what am I thinking, holding hands with him? But he just gives my hand a squeeze, like it's the most normal thing in the world. And maybe in this world, where nothing makes sense, it is.

I look around the room. Most of my classmates have moved back to their circle of sofas and chairs. I feel an emptiness, a hole where Mike should be, and for a moment it hurts so much it's hard to breathe. I close my eyes and will it to pass. When it does I look back at the circle. A few people, like Cassidy and Trevor, are talking in low voices but most of them just sit, slumped against each other, waiting for whatever comes next. Agents stand in every doorway watching us.

Hudson stands up, my hand slipping out of his as he does. "Let's get the phone," he whispers, glancing to see that no agents are close by.

I almost forgot about it but now that's he's reminded me I can't believe we've just been sitting around talking when the thing that will save us is still stuck in the sofa. Thankfully the agent who was sitting there is gone so we make our way over and I slip my fingers into the space between the cushions. But the phone has shifted, probably because of the weight of the agent who was sitting here. It's jammed under one of the cushions and I can't reach it.

"What's wrong?" Hudson asks, his voice taut. "Is it still there?"

"Yeah, but it's stuck."

"Can you get it without lifting the cushions?" he asks, his eyes on the agents.

"Yes."

There's no way I'm not getting my hands on the phone but I hear what he's saying about not being conspicuous. I think for a second, then bend down like I need to adjust my shoe and stick my hand under the cushion. This time I manage to get the phone and slide it into my sleeve.

"Got it?" he asks, still watching the guards.

"Yeah." I sit back against the oversized cushion, letting my head fall back.

He sighs. "Okay, so now we just wait to give it to Nico."

"Yeah." I say, rubbing my eyes, which are gritty from tears and being up so late. Fatigue suddenly feels like a heavy blanket falling over me.

"You know what I don't get?"

"What?"

"Why they haven't taken anyone out, like a new hostage, to call his or her parents or whatever," he says, his voice intense. "I mean, now that Mr. Barett is dead, how are they going to get money?"

He has my full attention now. "Maybe they're calling some of the parents and don't need the kids there?" I say. "Like Cassidy's dad is a senator and Ravi's family is loaded. They could be calling either one of them right now."

"Yeah, but wouldn't it make more sense to have the kids call their parents, with a gun to their heads, pleading and stuff? Plus I'm guessing the senator has an unlisted number. It would be so much quicker to just have the kid call the parent's cell phone. Parents always pick up for their kids."

"Yeah, that does make more sense," I say slowly.

"And if they wanted my money, they'd need me to get a hold of my manager," Hudson goes on. His face folds the tiniest bit as he says this.

A feeling crawls over me, cold with icy fingers.

"They must have some other kind of plan," I say, trying to shake off the feeling. And then the obvious occurs to me. "Ariel's dad isn't the sole owner of his company. He owns it with his brother."

"So you think they might be trying to find him to get the money?"

"Yeah, I bet that's what they're doing," I say. "He loves Ariel. If he knows they have her, he'd do everything he can to help."

Hudson sighs. "Which is why they'll keep killing us off until they find her. They need Ariel."

I look down at the phone hidden under my sweater. "We're getting help before that happens."

"I hope so," he says.

"Since it's a famous rock star, a senator's daughter, and a bunch of super-rich kids being held, I think the police will move on this pretty fast, once they know about it," I say.

He grins wryly. "Good point." He rubs his thumb along his jaw line for a moment. "Who do you think is behind this?"

I shake my head. "Honestly it could be a lot of people. It's not like I know much about Mr. Barett's business but even I know he had a lot of enemies. He wasn't exactly a nice guy." I immediately light up with guilt. "I shouldn't say that, though, now that he's dead."

Hudson rolls his eyes. "Why is that a rule? It seems stupid that you have to pretend someone was awesome after he died, even if he was a jerk sometimes."

"When my grandmother died we all talked about her like she was a saint even though all she did was complain that my dad didn't visit her enough. But I think it made my dad feel good when we said nice things about her."

"I get that," he says. "Except wouldn't you rather be remembered for who you really were, not some perfect version of you that's not even real?"

There is a heavy pause and I know he's thinking the same thing I am. This is the kind of conversation I'd have sometimes with Ariel, late at night when the lights were off and it felt like we were the only two people in the world. But this is different because here, in this room guarded at every door, in this room where we've seen four people get killed, dying isn't just hypothetical.

"Yeah, I think I'd want to be remembered for me," I answer. "Though honestly there wouldn't even be much to remember. I mean, I went to school and did some extracurriculars and that's about it."

"That's stupid," Hudson says, running his hands through his hair in that way I'm starting to love, though not as much in this moment when he just insulted me. "Who you are isn't about what you do. It's about your connections with people."

And I remember I'm talking to a guy who writes songs that cut straight to my soul.

"You mean who you love," I say. And the person who comes into my mind is Ariel. I've spent these past months feeling so badly that I told about Mexico, knowing that I let her down. But even if telling people was the wrong thing, for the first time I realize I don't regret it. "I'd be remembered for ratting out Ariel's secret. But I think I'm okay with that. Even if she hated me for it, I did it to try and help her." I pause for a second, then take a breath. "I did it because I loved her."

Something in the way Hudson is looking at me sends shivers down my spine. I look away, reminding myself this is not just some guy, this is a rock star and I am definitely seeing things that aren't there.

"I'll be discovered as a total fraud who lied to get famous," he says gloomily. "That's how I'll be remembered."

"Don't be insane," I tell him. "You'll be remembered for your songs. I love your music, honestly it's what got me through those first weeks after Ariel made everyone hate me."

He looks shocked. "Really?"

"Yeah. I mean, you have serious fans and it's not because they think you're hot. Your music means something to people."

He is now smiling just a bit too smugly. I shouldn't have said that part about him being hot.

"You like my music," he says, sounding like a kid who's just been given an ice cream cone.

"I love it. But don't let it go to your head."

He is about to say something but then he checks his watch and his face seems bathed in shadow. "We have to go," he says, standing up. "Nico's going to be there in a second."

I stand up too fast and then have a moment when I swoon, too light-headed to stand.

Hudson grabs me before I can fall. "Careful."

I can't help but notice how good he smells, like warm coffee and clean T-shirts right out of the dryer. I step away as soon as I can.

"Thanks, I'm fine. Let's go."

Nico is in the doorway of the kitchen when we get there, shifting his weight from one foot to the other. At least I assume the guy in the ski mask is Nico because it's our meeting spot. When he sees us he straightens and waves us over, giving a brief nod to the two agents standing in the far doorway.

We walk over to him. Hudson stands behind me, blocking me from view as I ease the phone out from my sleeve. For a terrible moment it is in the open, visible if anyone walked by, but Nico palms it, sliding it quickly into his pocket. Then he is gone.

I am limp with relief. We did it, we actually got him the phone.

We are going to be saved.

CHAPTER 18

Ariel

My uncle Marc is the one behind this, the one responsible for each person who has been shot in my home. I lean against the wall of the tunnel going back through this night, knowing what I now know. Marc and my dad started Barett Pharmaceuticals together but now Marc is barely involved and I'm assuming a good chunk of the money is unavailable to him. So if he wanted the money, he had to get my dad to sign things over to him. And to get my dad to do that Marc would need to put a huge amount of pressure on my dad, pressure like kidnapping him and taking a house full of kids hostage.

I have to admit, if that was his plan, he organized it well. Normally my dad would be nearly impossible to kidnap—he has too many enemies to go unguarded and he brings his security with him every time he leaves the house. But this party would have been a window of opportunity. My dad had to hire all kinds of extra security for Hudson, and Marc probably volunteered to be in charge of it. That way he could hire this band of psychopaths to hold us hostage while he got what he needed out of my dad. Plus Marc would know my dad's code for his safe and all kinds of other inside stuff he probably needs to take my dad's billions.

Though that doesn't quite add up because he was having me taken out of the room too. Maybe he was going to hold a gun to my head to force my dad to sign things over? My stomach is cold, like I swallowed too much ice, because I can't help wondering if a gun to my head would have been enough to get my dad to give up his life's dream and life's savings. That's probably why Marc had to take everyone else hostage too. Having a roomful of kids related to some of my dad's most important colleagues would certainly put the pressure on, if just my life wasn't enough. I put my hands on my stomach but it doesn't help so I stand up and head for my bedroom.

I can't believe my uncle would actually do this. And the more I think about it, the faster the cold creeps away, replaced by the burn of anger, which I like a lot better. By the time I reach my room I'm pretty much furious and hell-bent on taking Marc down. My guilt at Mike's death is still burrowed into a soft place at the center of my chest, but now that I know who did it, I can't let him get away with it. There will be no mansion in Brazil or a private island for Marc, not if I have anything to say about it. And thanks to Sera getting my dad's phone, I do.

Nico is in my room, pacing as he waits for me. I open the grate as fast and quietly as I can, and he turns as I walk in.

"Do you have it?" I ask.

His somber expression has me worried but then he reaches into his pocket and hands me the precious phone. Something loosens in me as I wrap my fingers around it, its sleek surface full of promise.

"You should go into the tunnels to call, so no one hears you," he says. His voice is flat.

"Right, I know," I say, walking back toward the fireplace. But then I stop. It isn't like him to look so somber, to be so quiet. And he hasn't smiled at me once. "What's wrong?"

He is silent for a moment, then shakes his head. "I'm sure it's nothing. Just something I will follow up on."

He looks at me and after a moment he smiles. He really does have a beautiful smile. I can't believe I never noticed it before. Which is an insane thing to be thinking right now.

"Okay, well, be ready for the police to come," I say quickly, stepping inside the dim space in the wall. I glance back at him.

"You should probably hide out somewhere until I can tell the police that you aren't one of the ones holding us hostage. I don't want you to get caught up in any of the arrests."

That smile again. "I will do that. Good luck."

I hear a noise in the hallway and I pull the grate in behind me, then walk into the tunnels.

The phone is all the luck I need and I focus on that, not my weird reaction to Nico that is probably just sleep deprivation. I walk about ten feet inside the tunnels, hopefully not too deep to lose cell phone reception. I press the phone to life and the silent request for a code lights up the screen. I tap in Swann161 and wait, ready for the menu to open, my fingers itching to dial 911. But what floats up instead are the words "access denied."

I bite back a scream of frustration. My dad was always saying he needed more than one password but I know this is the one he used for his most important things, the one he hasn't changed in the past ten years. Yet now, at this most crucial time, he opted to make a change on the one device that would have saved me. The burning in my stomach is creeping up to my throat but I take a deep breath and think. I can figure out his password if I just put my mind to it. He's not that creative, I know him well enough to crack this.

I close my eyes for a second to focus and then I start typing.

Twenty minutes later the phone flashes a warning that its battery is low and it is about to shut down. I turn it off to save its last bit of juice but there's no reason to, not really. I can't figure out my dad's password. Nothing works and I've tried absolutely everything. Once it's gone dark I slide the useless phone into my pocket and lower my head into my hands. I try to hold onto my fury, at my dad for changing his password and at Marc for starting this whole horror show. But it's slipping away, lost in the emptiness that is rising up like a windstorm inside me.

How could I not be able to figure out my own father's password? I know the answer of course. It's because I barely knew him and that was not my choice, it was his. Yeah, I stopped begging for scraps of his attention years ago when I developed some dignity, but I never stopped wanting it. But my dad always had other things, work things that came first. I told myself he was driven by money, that he was doing it for me and Abby, but the truth was always there, lodged like a splinter I could never tease out. I wasn't enough, not interesting or smart or good enough for him. If I had somehow been better, I would not be sitting alone in a tunnel, waiting for more of my friends to be shot at my birthday party.

Tears trickle down my face and I realize I am making a sound, a pathetic whimpering that I can't seem to stop. I press my hands over my mouth to try and keep the sound from traveling. I hate Marc and I hate my dad but most of all I hate that I never, not once, measured up.

I am vaguely aware of a rustling noise, like quiet footsteps, but since I don't really care what happens to me, I ignore it. But then Nico is there, his voice murmuring softly in Spanish as he pulls me close.

In a small part of my mind it occurs to me that I should pull away, that I don't want him to see me melt down like this, but I can't. It feels so good, so safe to be in his arms. So I just sink into him, letting him hold me while I cry and cry.

CHAPTER 19

Sera

I am in that glazed place between sleep and awake when Hudson's whole body goes tense next to me. I fumble to sit up and see what's caused his reaction, and then my heart smacks sickeningly against my ribs because I realize an agent is bearing down on us. I don't want to know what he wants because whatever it is, I don't think I can deal with it. Where are the police? Shouldn't they be here by now?

But when the agent comes close I realize that it's Nico. He sits down on the coffee table in front of us, hands on his knees, and leans in close. "There's a problem," he says softly. "I need you to come with me. Look scared and move fast because I have no idea what I'm going to say if someone stops us."

A problem and no excuse if we're stopped means looking scared is not exactly going to be a stretch. Hudson's mouth is taut, his hands tightened into fists, and I'm sure I don't look much calmer as we follow Nico briskly out into the hall.

We are silent as we go up the stairs at a near run, but luck is with us and we don't pass any agents on our way to Ariel's room. Nico goes in first, then Hudson, who pauses for a moment just inside the doorway. When I walk in I see why. Ariel is sitting on the ruined sofa, her face red and blotchy, her eyes hopeless.

"The phone doesn't work," Hudson guesses flatly.

"It works fine," Ariel says, her voice gravelly, like her throat is sore. "I just can't crack the code."

A rush of sympathy takes me by surprise. It's been a long time since I felt bad for Ariel but there it is. I know how much it crushed her that her dad never spent time with her and I know she thinks that's why she can't crack his password.

"You know, my mom tried for days to guess my dad's password," I say. "And she couldn't do it until he gave her all these hints."

Her eyes well with tears at my words and I glance at Nico, worried. Ariel is never this vulnerable. But he is looking at her, his face tender.

"So what do we do now?" Hudson asks. He is standing by the mantel over the fireplace drumming his fingers on the wood, his features dark.

That's when it hits me that we are completely screwed. I was so surprised by Ariel that I lost track of the fact that we can't call 911. I stagger over to the desk chair next to the sofa and fall into it. This is a disaster.

Ariel leans back as one of the tears spills over and slips down her cheek. "I don't know," she says. "But I do know who's behind this. My uncle Marc."

Her face is blank but I hear in her voice how much this hurts her. I think back to the few times I've met her fun-loving uncle. He bought Ariel a cotton candy machine for her tenth birthday and we got sick on a weekly basis 'til it finally broke. Do guys who buy cotton candy machines really take people hostage and commit murder?

"Are you sure?" I ask.

"As sure as I can be." Her shoulders slumped defeatedly. "I heard him saying some stuff in the hall."

"What stuff?" Hudson asks intently.

"What does it matter?' Ariel sighs. "Nothing that can help us, just enough to know that my own uncle is willing to kill me for money."

She sounds utterly beaten down but Hudson doesn't seem to notice. "The agents downstairs are going to kill a lot of us, not just you, if we don't figure out something to stop them."

Ariel looks at him, a tiny flicker of fire in her eyes. "Yeah, I know. And one of those people is going to be my six-year-old sister because I can't do anything to warn my ex-stepmother not to bring her here."

"Oh, no," I say.

"Yes," she says, and this time the pain is carved across her face.

"It gets worse," Nico says.

It's the first time he's spoken and we all turn toward where he is standing near the doorway, though I don't want to hear what he is going to say. Really, how much worse could this get?

"I got word from someone in the office suite," he says slowly. "They've managed to liquidate all the funds they can, but they can't leave until they have Ariel."

"You mean until they kill me," she says flatly.

"That I am not sure," Nico says. "But it is safe to assume."

"So what are they going to do if they don't find me?"

"They are starting the money transfer into a Swiss bank account. They think it will be done around six A.M. and that is when they are going to kill everyone."

The words crackle like an electric shock through the air.

"Wait, so they're just going to kill us all?" I ask in a voice that doesn't sound like me.

"Yes," Nico says. "They're going to burn the house down with everyone trapped inside."

Ariel closes her eyes. "I'll just turn myself in now. It's really the only thing to do."

We all start to speak at once until Hudson raises a hand. "That's not the answer. After all that's gone wrong they'd probably burn the house down no matter what, to erase as much of their trail as they can."

"He's right," Nico agrees. "Really that may have been the plan the whole time, to kill everyone in a fire."

The horror of this seeps into me. We are not going to get out of here alive.

"So, what, we just sit here and wait to be killed?" Ariel asks.

"Obviously not," Hudson says irritably. "We have to fight back."

"Are you carrying a stash of machine guns I wasn't aware of?" Ariel asks bitingly. "Because short of that, I'm not sure how we fight back."

"I don't mean we start some kind of epic battle," Hudson says. "I just mean we put up enough of fight that we can escape."

I try to find my voice but it's stuck inside my chest. I can't get past the thought of being burned alive before the sun rises.

"That sounds easy," Ariel says sarcastically, starting to sound more and more like herself, or at least herself when she is annoyed.

"So you want to just give up?" Hudson is close to yelling and Nico glances out the door, then gives Hudson a "shut up" look.

Hudson nods, acknowledging but still looking pissed at Ariel.

"Obviously that's not what I'm saying," Ariel says with a signature eye roll. "I want to take Marc down more than anyone. I'm just saying we need a plan."

"Agreed," Hudson says shortly. "So who has ideas?"

The room is silent. I can't seem to get my mind to work right, I just keep going over the things we've already said, like how Abby is coming and Marc is behind this and we're all going to be killed. That last part especially.

I look at Ariel. Her blond hair is tangled and even though she has a bit of her spark back she still looks tired and beaten, a lot like she did when she first came back from Mexico. And then something connects.

"In Mexico," I say. "Those guys who attacked you, do you think maybe it wasn't just a random attack or rape attempt or whatever?"

Ariel sits up, her body moving slowly. "You mean, is it possible they were trying to kidnap me and hold me hostage?"

"Yeah."

She is quiet, thinking. I see Hudson and Nico exchange a look but we all wait for Ariel.

"Yeah, I think that is possible," she says finally. "I bet that was Marc's first attempt to get my dad to give him everything. After that my dad tightened security for both of us so Marc had to wait for just the right opportunity to try again."

"And this was it," I say.

Hudson is looking at Ariel intently. "I know it sucks to think about it but is there anything, anything at all that you remember from it that might help us now?"

She pauses, then shakes her head. "Nothing comes to mind but I'll think about it."

It somehow changes things to know that Marc tried this before. I am guessing it makes him all the more determined to see it through this time.

"Okay, so now we need a plan," Nico says. "I say we keep it simple. We gather any weapons we can, Ariel leaves them somewhere you guys can get them, and we all fight our way out."

"We fight our way out against a bunch of armed agents?" Hudson asks skeptically.

"Honestly most of these guys would be reluctant to actually kill a bunch of kids," Nico says. "It's just the leader who's kind of trigger happy. Everyone else just wants to get paid and move on."

"So you think if we catch them by surprise we have a chance?" Hudson asks.

Nico nods. "They'll hesitate to do real damage and if we have some makeshift weapons, it could be enough to buy us the time we need to escape."

"What kind of weapons?" Ariel asks.

At the same time Hudson says, "Where will she leave them?"

Clearly they're sold on the plan and it makes sense to me too.

"There's a grate in the downstairs bathroom that's a door to the tunnel," Ariel says, answering Hudson's question. "I'll put stuff there, though I'm not sure what kind of weapons we have just lying around."

"Get creative," I say. "Like there's tons of beauty stuff that's lethal—hair spray and nail polish remover."

Ariel grins the tiniest bit. "I'd definitely run from a spray bottle with nail polish remover in it."

Hudson is starting to pace a little. "Those are really good ideas," he says. I can't help but grin at the compliment. "And anything sharp."

"We have an antique letter opener that's like a dagger," Ariel says. "And my dad has a Swiss Army knife. I'll get those."

"I have a Swiss Army knife too," I say, remembering.

"If it's with your overnight bag they brought those to the office suite," Nico says regretfully.

I smile, thinking of how sorry I felt for myself when I hung onto my overnight bag, knowing that someone in the class might dump it in a bathtub full of beer or something if they found it. Now it turns out my pariah status worked in my favor.

"No, it's behind the couch in the living room. I have a travel bottle of hair spray in there too."

"Excellent," Hudson says, so gleefully we all laugh until Nico gestures to be quiet.

"Okay, gather all the stuff you can and leave it in the tunnel inside the bathroom grate," Hudson says. "We'll figure out a way to get everything right before we start. In the meantime we need to convince everyone to go along with this."

Any last scraps of laughter fade with that remark, at least for me. Getting my classmates to just talk to me, let alone believe me, is not going to be easy. It's possible they'll listen to Hudson but he's been hanging out with me so much that he might be contaminated now too.

"And I'll organize everyone I can too," Nico says. "We'll time it so we all start at once."

"They're planning to start the fire at six so let's start at five," Hudson says.

"Okay," Nico agrees, looking at the clock. "That gives us two and a half hours to get ready."

Hudson looks at the clock too. "Two hours and thirty-seven minutes. We need to be exact."

"Right," Nico says, though Ariel is rolling her eyes.

Under other circumstances I might agree that he's being uptight but not now, not with all that hangs in the balance.

"We'll have to figure out the details of what we'll do, how we'll start our side of the fight," Hudson says to me. "But I think we have an overall plan."

"Yes, and now I need to get you both back," Nico says.

"I'll start collecting weapons," Ariel says as we head for the hall. She is walking toward the entrance to the tunnels. "I'll have them waiting for you within the hour."

"Sounds good," I say, and for a moment our eyes lock. There's probably a lot to say but there's no time, so I turn and follow Hudson and Nico.

As I go I wonder if I will ever see her again.

CHAPTER 20

Ariel

It turns out it's fun to scavenge for weapons. I am looking at the stuff in my house in this whole new, totally insane way, wondering what kind of damage it can inflict. Like the chunky marble bookends from my dad's bedroom. When thrown with force they could do real damage. And I'm all about doing damage right now.

The best part is there's no room to think. I am too busy analyzing the tray in the guest room that has razor sharp edges and gathering up the scissors from the den utility drawer. With my mind full of things like this I can't speculate on what has happened and what might happen next.

I haul the bookends, scissors, and my dad's vintage golf clubs (I decided against the tray—it's square and awkward to hold). It's a small load but heavy because of the marble and golf clubs. I'm stocking up everything I find upstairs, then I'll take it downstairs and start scavenging the rooms there. I already have a bounty of spray bottles filled with toxic beauty and cleaning supplies from my bathroom as well as the razor blades from my dad's. I also include a can of shaving cream—it's not dangerous to breathe but it would be blinding and that could be useful in a tight spot.

My last upstairs stops are my bedroom and the back guest suite. I head for my bedroom first and pause at the fireplace to make sure no one's in there. When I see it's empty I feel the tiniest sting of disappointment. I tamp it down fast but really it's too late and I have to admit it, at least to myself, I was hoping Nico would be here.

I know my weird reaction to him these past hours is probably just some kind of backlash from the stress but I can't deny that I feel safer when he's around. Actually that makes sense because he's probably a pretty good bodyguard. It's the sweet, fizzy feeling

I get when I think about how his eyes crinkle when he smiles at me, his eyes like honey in the sun, that is just ridiculous. So I do what I can to shove it aside and force my mind back to weapons and slide soundlessly into my bedroom. Of course a lot of my stuff was destroyed in the room itself so I head to the closet. Clothes have been thrown to the floor but most of the other things, including my endless racks of shoes, are untouched. I look at the shoes, analyzing, then grab two pairs of strappy, pointy stilettos. You could easily take out someone's eye with the heel of one of these.

I get out the step stool and climb up to look at the shelves above my clothes. It's mostly books and boxes of old papers, pictures from when I was little and stuff. I generally avoid looking at it because it's depressing to think neither of my parents saved it so I had to save it myself, but now I look it over, just in case there's anything in there that could cause damage. But books aren't dangerous enough, not unless you sit down and read some of them, so I am about to climb back down when I notice a book I don't recognize. It's at the other end of the closet so I have to get down, move the step stool, and then climb back up.

When I do, I expect to pick it up and then remember what it is, but that doesn't happen. It's a big book with a red leather cover and I'd swear I've never seen it before. I am just about to open it when I hear footsteps in the hall. I freeze, but after a moment they pass. I climb down quickly, the red book tucked under my arm, and head back for the tunnels. I'll look at it there, where I can't be discovered.

I replace the grate behind me, then walk until I am near a grate in the hall where enough light spills in that I can see what the book is. I can also overhear something if anyone passes by.

I sit down and lean against the wall, realizing how tired I am. It's the kind of exhaustion that seeps into my bones, heavy and numbing. It's not just that it's late because plenty of weekends I am at parties 'til after three A.M. It's what the creepy shrink I saw would call "emotional fatigue." I rub my eyes trying to brush it off. Then I open the book.

It's a photo album and the first page is baby pictures. It takes me a second to realize that the baby in them is me. Me on a yellow blanket wearing a onesie with a duck on it, me on the beach in a big green sunhat, me asleep on my mom's shoulder, my little bald head tucked snug against her. On the next page I am sitting up, then crawling, in every picture a big smile on my face for the person holding the camera. In most of the shots it must be my mom, but in the ones where we are together I realize it's possible that my dad is the one shooting the pictures.

Why haven't I ever seen these before?

I am on the page with my kindergarten graduation (NCCD does it big so I am decked out in a one-of-a-kind designer dress) when I hear voices in the hall. I kneel by the grate to see who it is and if I can catch any scraps of conversation but the two men walking by are silent when they pass. One is an agent, the other is Owen Davis, John's assistant. I didn't even know he was here tonight. He must have been up in the office suite working, which is not at all unusual for a Saturday night. What bad luck for Owen to be here on *this* Saturday night.

After they pass I go back to the photo album, flipping through pages of me growing older, on the beach at St. John's when I was seven, skiing in the Alps at ten, the trip to the Cannes film festival when I was thirteen. The older I get, the less I am smiling in the pictures. I get to the last page, which is a few shots from our last family vacation before my mom died, when we went to New Zealand and I wouldn't even look at the camera. I vaguely remember my parents trying to get me to pose (during the few moments my dad looked up from his computer or wasn't on the phone) but I had just started going out with Leo Chan, a junior and the center on the basketball team, and I was angry to be so far away from him over break. In fairness rightly so because he dumped me when I got back to go out with another junior whose family stayed home over break, whom he probably made out with at all the parties while I was gone. But now I kind of regret that I spent that whole trip in such a bad mood.

I am about to close the album and get on with my weapons search when I notice the back cover has a panel in it, almost like a folder, and there is something in there. It's a thick document and when I take it out I am shocked to see it's a copy of my dad's will. What is it doing in here? Did my dad leave it in my closet for me to find? I honestly, that is the only explanation I can think of but it makes no sense because there's no reason for him to want me to have a copy of it. And if he did want me to have it, why not just give it to me, why hide it?

I massage my temples, wishing my head didn't feel like it was stuffed with cotton from my exhaustion. Every thought feels sluggish and hard to conjure up but I push myself because there has to be a reason that this album, with the will, was left in my closet.

My mind drifts back to what Sera asked me, about whether what happened in Mexico was a kidnapping attempt. As soon as she said it I knew she was right. I assumed attack and rape or whatever, but they never tried to take my clothes off and though they did beat me up, it was more to subdue me, not to inflict serious damage. Just the fact that I have no scars, at least the kind you can see, proves that. What I remember is that they came in, hit me 'til I stopped fighting, tied me up, and threw me down on the floor. I assumed that the rape would have come next if the police hadn't barged in at that moment, but what if they were really getting ready to take me somewhere to hold me hostage? It makes a lot more sense and if I'd ever allowed myself to think about that day, I'd probably have realized it before. And my dad, who probably thought about it plenty, most likely realized it too.

After Mexico my dad got us both bodyguards around the clock and gave me a big lecture about being more careful. I assumed it was because he didn't want his oldest daughter getting raped but it was more likely that he didn't want to risk losing his fortune if I got kidnapped. It's heartwarming to realize his concern was more for his money than me and I'm starting to get angry about that when I notice the album next to me, the whole reason I'm thinking about all of this in the first place. I settle myself down and focus.

If I am going to assume my dad thought Mexico was a kidnapping attempt and that he put this album in my closet for me to find, it must have been something he thought I'd need if something like Mexico happened again, but this time to him. After all, he beefed up his own security so he must have known we were both vulnerable. So even though there are copies of this will in his office and in his lawyer's office—and that's when I gasp.

Mr. Black died four weeks ago in a car crash and all of a sudden I realize it might not have been an accident after all. I remember my dad that night he came back from Mr. Black's funeral, how remote he was until Marc cheered him up. Did he suspect that Mr. Black was murdered?

I'm probably going off the deep end but the more I think about it, the more I believe I'm onto something. My dad's lawyer must have had documents that would make it hard for Marc to transfer the money to himself, so the lawyer had to go. And if my dad left me the will, then the will has to be one of those documents, something that could somehow impede Marc. I hunker down and read.

It's on the second page. I always assumed my dad would leave the company to Marc or have it sold to the board members with the money going to Abby and me. My dad made decisions based on a business bottom line and that would be the best business choice, to pass the company on to someone who could run it in the most money-making way possible, carrying on my dad's name and legacy while at the same time providing handsomely for his daughters. And really I never gave it much thought. I knew I'd have enough money that I could pursue whatever I felt like pursuing and what my dad did with his company was his call. Now, seeing the choice he made, has my eyes getting watery and my chest getting tight. Because my dad didn't make the best business decision at all.

The person he named sole heir to Barett Pharmaceuticals is me.

CHAPTER 21

Sera

"So how do we do this?" Hudson asks.

We've just gotten back to the game room and it's time to get my classmates onboard with our plan, a task that seems even more daunting than escaping the agents. We are lurking by the sofa where no agents can overhear us, looking at my NCCD classmates who are in their spots on the sofas, a few people asleep, everyone else looking about halfway there. They are not going to welcome us into that circle.

"I'm not sure," I say. My mouth is dry and chalky and my breath probably smells atrocious. I can't convince anyone to believe me with breath like this. "I need some water and then we can figure it out."

The agent who usually guards this doorway is out in the hall and he or she nods when we ask if it's okay to go get a drink.

"I think we start by convincing one person," Hudson says softly as I fill a glass from the big bottle of imported French water on the wooden stand by the sink.

"That makes sense but we have to wait for a chance to get someone alone," I say, automatically checking that the agents in the doorway are too far away to hear. "Maybe we stake out the bathroom."

I lift the glass to my lips and drink about half of it down in one gulp.

Hudson laughs, then wrinkles his nose. "You don't want ice with that?"

"I hate cold water," I tell him, refilling my glass.

"You're weird," he says in this affectionate tone that makes my heart a little fluttery. I take a long drink of water to focus firmly on reality.

I turn and see Franz and Ella walk in. They kind of glance at Hudson as they head over to the fridge. Franz's eye is swollen and tender-looking but one of the guys gave him an undershirt so he's no longer wearing a blood-soaked shirt.

Hudson and I exchange a look—this is our shot.

"Can we talk to you guys for a second?" I ask, going over to them so that the agents in the doorway don't overhear.

Now they are the ones exchanging a look and I wish I hadn't asked, that I'd just started talking.

"It's important," Hudson says, joining us.

There's no denying the rock star power, not when he smiles that famous smile. They both nod, their faces practically lit up by his glow.

"We've been talking to some people and the situation has gotten really bad," I say softly, double-checking that the agents in the doorway can't overhear. But they are speaking quietly to each other and don't seem interested in our conversation. "The agents aren't going to let us go."

For a moment my words don't really register but then Ella's brow creases. "Wait, what?"

"They're not going to let us go, not after all that's gone wrong," Hudson says.

Ella looks alarmed but Franz raises an eyebrow skeptically. It's hard to be convincing when we can't explain about Ariel.

"There's an agent who's on our side," I say, hoping they don't ask for more information about him. "He says that at this point the guy in charge has to erase all the evidence of this night and that includes us."

"If they ever even meant to let us go," Franz says. I realize he wasn't skeptical before, he was thinking we were slow on the uptake.

"Right," Hudson says. "And we're not just going to sit around and wait to die. We're going to fight."

"And take down a bunch of trained and armed assassins? I don't think so." Now Franz *is* skeptical.

"It's not so much about taking them down as it is catching them by surprise so we can escape," I explain. "We have someone who is going to get weapons for us, unconventional ones like letter openers, and we'll come up with a plan and—"

"What's going on?" One of the agents from the doorway has taken notice of our talk and is walking over.

Franz's face is a mask of fear and Ella looks pale.

"She's not feeling well," I say quickly. "We're just trying to figure out how to help."

The agent scrutinizes Ella who looks like she is about to puke, so my story is believable.

"Just go back to the living room and deal," he says shortly.

We are quick to head out.

"Can you talk to the others, convince them that we all need to work together?" Hudson whispers as we go.

Franz nods once, his face still tight. He and Ella walk back over to the group while Hudson and I go to our spot in the far corner of the room.

"I don't think that went so well," I say once we are sitting down.

"He agreed to try to convince the others," Hudson says, but he sounds worried too. "Let's just assume he's successful and start figuring out a plan."

"Okay." That's a better idea than just sitting around stressing about what my classmates will say.

"We're going to have trouble all talking together so it probably makes sense to pick like three leaders who can all meet and then spread the word," he says, drumming his fingers on his knee.

"That's a good idea and we should probably have them each be in charge of a specific group of people," I say, thinking of Field Day in eighth grade when our team won thanks to what we called the multipronged attack. "That way we can form an attack plan with different groups doing different things, like one group staging a distraction and another group attacking from behind or whatever."

"And the third group working on getting an escape route." He grins at me. "You're good at this. Are you sure you don't have an Army background?"

The expression on his face is making my chest all fluttery and I am fumbling for an answer when his face suddenly tightens at something he sees over my shoulder. I whip my head around, expecting an agent, but instead it's something worse. Cassidy is heading right for us and she is furious.

"Listen up," she hisses sitting down on the coffee table in front of me and leaning in so close that I move back instinctively. "I don't know if you're just trying to screw with us or what but stop."

Hudson starts to speak and she raises a hand as she turns her poisonous gaze at him. "I don't know what our backstabbing friend here has told you but one of her many flaws, aside from being a spineless wimp, is a pathological need for attention. I'd suggest you assume everything she says is a lie and move on."

In just a few short phrases she has laid me bare. My faults are like worms under a log that has just been turned over, squirming and disgusting in the light. My eyes fill with tears and I duck my head.

There is a pause and I think we are both waiting for Hudson's response but he says nothing. He probably agrees with everything she said. But when I finally look up I can tell from how stiff his spine is and the way his lips are pressed together that he hates what she said. So why isn't he defending me?

But then he looks at me and I know. I can't stand up for myself in a room full of agents if I can't face down this, this hatred and disdain that has clung to me for the past nine months and four days. And let's face it, if I'm going to die, I want to do it with my spine fully intact.

"You're wrong," I say.

She arches an eyebrow at me. "Am I now? About what exactly?"

She wants to bait and trap me but it's not going to happen. "I told about what happened to Ariel in Mexico because I was scared she was going to kill herself," I say. "I didn't know what else to do."

Cassidy recoils, unsure how to respond because instead of attacking her or getting defensive, stuff she is a pro at shredding, I was honest, and she has no idea how to deal with that. So I keep going.

"I wish it didn't make her hate me but I'm not sorry I did it," I say. "Because she got help and she really, really needed it."

"Okay," Cassidy says, drawing out the word because she's not sure what else to say. Before she can get back on her game I continue. "And that's what we need to do now," I say in a rush. "Help each other because I swear, Cassidy, these guys are not going to let us go and I don't want to die here tonight."

Saying it like that makes me choke up because it's so achingly true. I can't fathom this night being the very last of my life.

"There's no way they're letting us go," Hudson says quietly. "Our only options are to let them slaughter us or fight for our lives. Fight with us, please."

She is quiet and I hear the crackle of the fire in the fireplace. I don't think about how much rests on what Cassidy says next, I just let myself feel the lightness that came when I finally stood up for myself. If this is my last night, at least I can feel good about that.

"I believe you," she says finally, glancing to make sure no agents are close. "We'll fight."

Hudson's eyes are shining as he reaches over and grabs my hand. It's insane that even in this moment his touch sends shivers down my whole body.

"Okay," he says. "This is what we're thinking."

He starts telling her about the idea for leaders and what he is now calling platoons and soon the three of us are strategizing, making the plan that maybe, just maybe, will save us.

CHAPTER 22

Ariel

I can't stop crying. Not the out of control sobbing of before but tears that drip down my face, my insides achy, my throat raw. I can't believe my dad left me his company. Barett Pharmaceuticals was everything to him and that he would entrust it to me, that he thought I was worthy of taking it over for him, by myself— I can't even wrap my mind around it. Because he would only leave the company to someone he had utmost respect for, whom he believed was smart enough and tough enough and good enough—and now it turns out that person was me.

I think of all the times he blew me off for business dinners, all the performances he missed because meetings went late or he had to travel. But now it's like I'm seeing it from a whole other perspective because the company isn't just his baby, my rival. The company is something he was building up to give to me. All of a sudden all those meetings and dinners he went to, all the things that kept him from being with me, seem like acts of love. Because this whole time he was getting it ready to pass it on to me.

I pick up the album and page through it again, careful not to let my tears drip all over it. This album was my dad's, I know that now. He kept it in his room and that's why I never saw it before. He looked through it, maybe late at night after those meetings, because it made him happy to see pictures of me. Because he loved me. This whole time he loved me.

It's not until I hear someone walk past, steps muffled on the hall carpet, that I finally pull myself together. I have work to do. Now that I know the company was supposed to go to me, I am ready to fight, not just for my life but for my dad's legacy and my future. Marc is not draining that company, not after all my dad—and I—sacrificed for it. That company is mine and I am going to hold onto it with everything I've got. Marc is not going to get away with this.

I stand up, my legs and lower back stiff, and stretch for a moment, then head toward the back guest suite. I'm going to finish up my weapons quest and then I'm going to figure out exactly how I'm going to take Marc down.

The grate for the guest suite is in the fireplace and the latch on this one is a little harder to open. It's rusted or something and I have to press down on it with both hands to get it to budge. I finally open it but it squeaks loudly and I stop, waiting to see if anyone has heard. After a few minutes I squeeze through the small space—I don't want to open it anymore and risk more noise.

The room is dark so I tiptoe over to the door and open it so light from the hallway streams in. Then I turn around and notice there is something on the bed. I walk closer and then freeze. The thing on the bed is a body. An agent is napping and I've walked right in, practically handing myself over to them.

But then I realize the body is unnaturally still. I walk closer, my heart now in my throat. When I get so close I can smell the salty, iron-like scent of blood I realize I am looking at a dead body. I reluctantly force my gaze up to the face and my legs give out. I crash down hard on my knees, a scream boiling in the back of my throat, my hands over my mouth to hold it in and to keep from puking.

Because the body on the bed, bleeding from a shot that has ripped half his head off, is my Uncle Marc.

CHAPTER 23

Sera

"Things are going to happen now," I say to Hudson as I watch Cassidy stride back to the group and start talking in a low voice.

"Good," Hudson says. "And I'm thinking now would be the time for you to get your bag so we can see what kind of stuff we can use as weapons. Where is it?"

"Right behind me." I wave my hand toward the back of the sofa where I stuffed my bag, back when I thought the worst thing I'd be facing down was my hostile classmates.

"Finally something easy," he says, but then he glances at the agent in the doorway to the kitchen who has a great view of us. "Or maybe not so much."

"If you turn toward me your back will block his view. Like we did with the phone."

"That was smaller. You don't strike me as a light packer."

"In this case you should be thanking me for that," I say. "Light packers don't bring bottles of hair spray with them."

"An excellent point," he says, with a lopsided grin. "But we still have the problem of how to get into the bag."

"I think it'll be okay. It's really not that big."

Hudson shifts so his body is blocking me from the agent's view and I reach behind the sofa and pull up the bag. I realize my hands are shaking when it takes me two tries to open the clasp but then it snaps open and I start rummaging around. I grab my toiletries bag—that is going to have the stuff we can use. Everything else is just clothes. Well, everything except the Swiss Army knife. I pull that out, then replace the bag behind the sofa and let out the breath I was holding.

I look over Hudson's shoulder at the agent. He is chatting with a second agent and neither of them is looking our way. "We're good."

I open the bag and peer in. There's the hair spray of course and also a nail file that might be useful, as well as the rinse I spritz on my hair before drying it. It's made from plants so it doesn't have the toxic advantage of the hair spray.

"Should we bother with this?" I ask Hudson.

He considers. "Yeah, I'm thinking anything you can spray in someone's face to get a few extra seconds is worth it."

That makes sense. "I think that's it. Where should we store it?"

He thinks for a moment. "Let's put it back with the other bag, but on top, where you can grab it easily when the time comes.

I do as he says and when I turn back around I see Cassidy waving at us from the poker table. Franz, Ravi, and Ella are already sitting around it.

"Looks like we're going to have our first meeting," I say, and Hudson twists around to see them.

"Great," he says, standing up and heading over.

I'm about to follow when I notice the Swiss Army knife still on the sofa—I didn't think to put it in the cosmetics bag. Without Hudson to block me I don't want to risk putting it with the bags so I slip it into my pocket as casually as I can and head over to the poker table.

"This is our leaders meeting," Cassidy says, picking up a deck of cards. "Disguised as a poker game."

Franz is setting out the wooden case of poker chips.

"Let's do it," Hudson says, pulling out a chair.

I do too, though hesitantly because I'm not sure if I should. I don't think I'm a leader.

Cassidy notices. "Do you both need to be here?" she asks, glancing from me to Hudson before shuffling the deck with such precision it makes a snapping sound, then dealing the cards with a tiny flick of her wrist.

"We stick together," Hudson says.

I feel a rush of warmth in my face and my whole body feels tingly. I take a breath to calm down and get grounded back in reality, reminding myself that this is a rock star making my pulse go nuts, not a regular guy. There is no shot at anything romantic happening, no matter how sexy he sounded when he said that.

Cassidy raises her eyebrows, though I can't tell whether it's in reaction to what Hudson said or her cards. "Got it." She slaps down two cards, deals herself two more, and moves on to Ravi who wants one new card. "This is the deal so far. Ravi's group is going to be in charge of staging some kind of distraction. My group will be the first line of attack, after they get the agents distracted, and Ella's group is going to come in right after us. Franz's group will be on the doorway to the kitchen since most of the agents seem to come in from there and they'll try to stop as many as they can. That leaves the two of you free to figure out how we get out of here. Everybody ante up."

I forgot we were supposed to be playing so I fumble for a moment to get my chips set and my cards fanned out. I have a bad hand but I suck at poker anyway so I don't bother trading in any cards.

Hudson is nodding. "Okay, we'll focus on taking out the guards at the doorway to the living room and clearing the way for you guys to follow us out to the front door."

I drop my chips on the table. That sounds impossible. But Cassidy gives me an arch look and I gather up my chips and my wits. We're all doing impossible things so I might as well just get past that and start thinking about the most direct route out of the Barett mansion.

"What kind of distraction are you guys going to stage?" Franz asks.

"I think Aisha will fake a seizure," Ravi says.

Aisha has had the lead in every play since we were in middle school and has already done bit parts on Broadway. She's perfect for that. Then I think of something.

"You know what, she should do it in the bathroom," I say. "That way maybe you can get some agents in there, sneak her out, and lock them in."

"I like that," Ravi says, giving me a thumbs up. "Maybe we can grab one of their guns in the confusion."

It's weird to have my classmates talking to me again.

"Yeah, it's smart," Cassidy agrees. "You'll just have to think it through carefully so that you get her out."

The thought of Aisha or any of us trapped in a room with agents is awful. "Yeah, that would be essential," I say.

"So are we just fighting them off with whatever skills we have or are we going to try and find weapons?" Ella asks. "They put away the sharp knives in the kitchen but maybe we can find some other stuff."

Hudson looks at me.

"We have a weapons source," I say slowly. "And we'll have some stuff hidden for us in the bathroom." I glance at the clock and see it's a little after four. "It's probably already there."

Cassidy looks at me through slitted eyes. "A *weapons source?*" she asks, her voice drenched in sarcasm.

"I think the less everyone knows about that, the better," Hudson says. "What matters is that we'll have some stuff, like hair spray and letter openers, that we can use."

Cassidy shrugs. I can tell by the crease in her forehead she's annoyed but she's letting it go and that's the important thing. Then she looks at me. "So what do you say?"

For a second I have no idea what she's talking about but then I realize it's my turn. "Oh, um, I'll fold."

"You can't fold, we have to all keep playing so the game looks real," she snaps.

"Right, okay, then I see your ten and raise you twenty," I say, shoving in my chips.

Hudson grins at me. "Sometime I want to play a real game with you. I'm guessing I'd take the house."

"You should challenge her to strip poker," Franz says.

I shoot him a look. I almost forgot Franz's sleazy French humor since I haven't been its target for the past nine months and four days. And I definitely haven't missed it.

"Not a bad idea," Hudson muses, grinning at me wickedly.

My face is on fire.

"Now that I think of it, what are we waiting for?" Franz asks. "Let's make this game about getting naked."

"Right, because us getting naked will totally not get the agents' attention," Ella says, rolling her eyes. "Only you could think of sex at a time like this."

"Actually he's not the only one," Ravi says, and he and Franz exchange a high-five.

"Let's focus," Cassidy says, but I can tell she is amused by the way the corners of her mouth turn up the slightest bit.

I forgot how much I used to like these people.

"So who will give the signal when it's time to start?" Hudson asks. He is grinning too.

"Ravi, since his group is making the first move," Cassidy says. "We should all be in our places, ready to grab weapons at 4:55."

No one is smiling now.

"I'll get the weapons at 4:30," I say. "Though we have to figure out how to get them out of the bathroom and hidden around the room."

"Maybe you go and take stock of what we have early," Cassidy says. "That way we know exactly what we have and we can plan for it. I call."

We spread our cards.

"Damn," Hudson says as Cassidy scoops up the pot. He had two aces but she had a full house.

Cassidy shuffles and deals us each a new hand. "See if you can hold your own this time, rock star," she says to Hudson.

He acknowledges the challenge with a raised eyebrow but then he glances at the clock and his face is solemn again. "Sera, you should probably go check on the weapons, unless you want me to do it."

"Sera does it because she knows the house best," Cassidy says without looking up.

Hudson raises his hands in submission but I can tell he gets a kick out of how bossy she is. Guys always do, even though any other girl who gets bossy is tagged with the bitch label. Cassidy is somehow immune to that and has guys falling at her feet when she orders them around. Which has me suddenly feeling jealous until Hudson squeezes my hand.

"Be careful," he says, his eyes intent on my face.

"She's just going to the bathroom," Cassidy huffs. "Save the melodrama for the actual fight."

I would laugh if the whole going to take stock of the weapons thing didn't have my insides wound taut. But it needs to be done so I stand up and walk over to the agent nearest the bathroom.

"Is it okay if I use the restroom?" I ask, shifting my weight from one leg to the other like I really need to go. Which is probably unnecessary but it helps me stay calm to fidget a little.

He or she nods, not even looking at me, so I walk in and close the door firmly behind me. I quietly open the grate. I peer in but don't see anything. Did she leave them farther down? I hoist myself up into the passageway and look in both directions. There's enough light from the grates down the narrow tunnels that I can see pretty far, and there are no weapons, not anywhere.

My insides twist into a tight coil, making it hard to breathe. There's something wrong. Ariel was supposed to have the weapons here by now and there's no way she'd just forget or be late, not with all that's at stake.

I hesitate, unsure what to do. If I go look for her, I'll be in the bathroom way too long and the agents will start knocking. But if I don't go, we don't have any weapons except the few things from my bag. And more than that, I'm worried about Ariel.

It goes against every instinct I have to steady the grate behind me and head off down the tunnels because I know it's my grave I'm digging. But really what choice do I have?

I secure the grate behind me and take off at a run.

CHAPTER 24

Ariel

I am curled up on the sofa in the blue room, not crying, not thinking, especially not about what Marc was holding in his lifeless hand. The blue room is off at the end of the back hall and it's the smallest room in the house. When I was little it was my favorite place to go when I was scared because it was the only place in my house you could call cozy, and the sofa and armchair in here are worn and comfortable, not sleek like the furniture in the rest of the house. I haven't been in here for a while but it's where I came, on autopilot, after I first saw my uncle's body. I didn't think any of the agents would bother coming in so I turned on a small lamp in the corner. I can't be in a dark room right now.

"Ariel," a voice whispers, making me leap up in the air. I fall back, half on the floor, and look around frantically but don't see anyone. Then the grate opens and Sera steps out, a cobweb in her hair from the tunnels.

"Sorry, I didn't mean to give you a heart attack," she says, coming and sitting on the chair across from me.

"How did you find me here?" There are a lot of things I could ask her right now but that is the thing that comes out.

"I know you better than you think," she says ruefully. "What's going on?"

I don't think I can talk about it without a meltdown so I stand up, proud to discover my shaky legs can support me. "Sorry about the weapons, I got sidetracked," I say. "But I have a lot of stuff. We can go get it now."

She says nothing, just tips her head and looks at me with those knowing, Sera eyes. And that's all it takes. I am back on the sofa, tears spilling out.

"Marc is dead," I manage to choke off before I start sobbing.

Her eyes go wide but instead of asking me what I'm talking about, she comes over, wraps her arms around me, and lets me cry. And cry I do. It must be five minutes before I'm able to pull myself together. And then I'm mortified.

"I think I'm going soft," I say, fumbling on the side table for a tissue to mop up my face.

"Right, two people in your family dead, a third in danger, and here you are, totally overreacting," she says.

I always love it when she brings the sarcasm. "Yeah, I guess, but falling apart doesn't help."

"Being human is allowed."

I should have a retort for that but I'm kind of running on empty. Plus she might be right. I stuff the dirty tissues in my pocket and sink down into the sofa.

"So what happened to Marc?" Sera asks.

"He was shot."

"I'm so sorry."

I really don't want to feel anything about Marc's death. I'm not even sure I'm allowed to feel bad after I spent all these hours thinking he's the one behind this hostage takeover. What kind of person suspects her uncle of something like that? Especially since he had my heart necklace in his hand when he died. Well, Bianca's, technically, but he would have thought it was mine and that is probably how they got him to do whatever they told him to. He did it to try and save me. I close my eyes, trying to ward off the image of the necklace clutched in his fingers.

"So this probably means he wasn't the one behind this whole thing," Sera says.

"No, I don't think so," I say, guilt tearing at me with small claws.

"Then who do you think is?" she asks.

I've been so busy not thinking about Marc that I haven't even started to wonder about this. But now that she says it, I can't believe I let it go this long.

"I don't know," I say, my spine straightening just a bit. "It has to be someone who knew my dad pretty well."

"And someone who was in a position to hire security for this," Sera says.

"He could have passed that off to any assistant," I say. "But for that person to know his safe combination . . . "

Sera looks at me blankly.

"I went to his bedroom and someone had opened his safe and cleared it out."

She rubs her thumb along her chin the way she does when she's thinking about something. "Yeah, but maybe whoever is behind this just put a gun to Marc's head and told him to open it."

"That's possible," I say, thinking of the conversation I overheard between Marc and the agent earlier tonight. They had a gun to his head then too, I was just too stupid to realize it.

Sera has moved on to hair twisting, a sure sign she is anxious about something. "It would also be someone who was there in Mexico."

Suddenly the elephant has walked into the room. It was one thing to mention Mexico when the guys were there but now it's just us and the elephant, big and bulky and impossible to get around.

Sera looks at me evenly. "I'm not sorry I told," she says. "I had to do something and that was the best I could do."

This is so not what I expected her to say. The few times she managed to talk to me or text me after it happened, all she did was apologize.

"You needed help," she adds.

I'm so going soft because here I am, tearing up again. "I know," I say, gulping a little. "And you were probably right to do it."

Now she is the one who looks surprised, shocked even. I can't believe I'm admitting that, to her or myself, but I know it's true.

"It was just, to have it out in the open like that, I couldn't take it," I say. "I'm sorry I was such a jerk about it."

This is weak and I know it but how do you apologize for something that's pretty unforgivable? I was angry about Mexico and I took it all out on Sera, the person least deserving of my wrath.

But Sera is just nodding. "Yeah, I get that."

She does not tell me it's okay because we both know it's not. But her getting it—that is a lot and I realize that something inside me that has been locked up tight is loosening just the tiniest bit.

"It was just so awful," I say brokenly. "I still have flashbacks about it every time I smell lemons or—"

"Wait." Sera's eyes widen. "Lemons?"

"Yeah, I think they used lemon-scented cleaner at the hotel in Mexico."

She cocks her head. "Or were they lemon lozenges?"

I draw a blank but then I get it. "No, John would never do this."

If there's one thing I know for sure, it's that John Avery could never be part of something this cruel. I was quick to think Marc was guilty and I'm not going to do the same thing here.

Sera puts her hand over mine. "Are you sure?" she asks gently. "I know John has been good to you over the years but he's always sucking those lemon lozenges and I think he might have been the one in charge of security for the party."

"What makes you think that?" I ask, narrowing my eyes.

Sera twirls a lock of hair around her fingers. "I just remembered it now but when I first got here, I was talking to your dad and John. Your dad was saying how all the guys in the garden with machine guns seemed like a lot of security for one singer and John said something like, well, that's what his people said he needed. And it made me think he was the one to hire the security."

"That doesn't prove anything," I say, though there is a thick smoke filling my chest. "He could have passed it on to anyone."

"True, but what if I'm right?"

"You're not," I say.

Now she reaches for my other hand. I try to pull them away but she must have been working out these past months because she has them in a death grip and is not letting go.

"I know it sucks to think about but please, for just one minute, consider that it could be John."

"Fine," I huff. Sure, I'll consider it and then decide it's wrong. And then I remember I have something that can answer this question once and for all. I pull my hands free and this time Sera lets me. I take the stapled pages out of my pocket and start to unfold them. "This is the plan my dad had for the party. It should say here who was in charge of security."

"Oh, good," Sera says. "And I apologize in advance if I falsely accused John."

My hands are shaking as I smooth down the pages. I set the plan on the table and start to read, Sera leaning over my shoulder, reading along with me. Her breath on my cheek, which is not exactly smelling good, should annoy me but somehow it's comforting me instead. I don't want to find this out alone.

The first page has typed details of the catering plan with my dad's notes in the margin. Things like "remember A doesn't like walnuts" make my throat tight. Page two details the concert. Hudson's rep said his bodyguard would accompany Hudson who asked that water be available before the concert. I guess he's not a diva the way some stars are with their requests of champagne and truffles. Suggested security is a minimum if seven guards on the property, dispersed between the yard and the house, and they are happy to supply the five if needed. I don't want to read what my dad has scrawled in the margin right next to that but I force my eyes over. "John will take over the hiring of security for the concert." The words draw blood.

A moment later Sera reads them. I can tell because she gasps and then starts rubbing my back in small circles, the way she did when my dad was a no-show at my birthday party last year.

"I'm sorry," she says.

"Yeah, me too."

We are quiet for a moment, then she clears her throat. "It's good we know."

"I guess," I say.

I mean, one of the few people I thought I could trust has turned out to have a death wish against me so it's hard to actually cheer for this news. But once I get past that I'll probably see that she's right. And that's probably when I'll start to get angry about it too. Right now, though, I just feel like I've been run over by an SUV.

"What's this?" Sera asks, pointing to a date my dad wrote on the bottom of the page. It's by the section labeled "Toast."

"It's the year of your birth but two days after your birthday," she continues.

"Right, that's the first day my dad met me," I say, thinking of how my mom used to talk about how I was early and my dad was in Japan when I was born. It took him over twenty-four hours to get to the hospital and—

"Oh, my God," I say, jumping up.

"What?" Sera asks, looking worried.

"I know!" I say excitedly. "I know what my dad's phone code is."

And then we hear a noise in the hall. I snatch up the party plan and we streak for the grate as two agents walk in.

"Who turned this light on?" one of them asks.

The other shrugs. "Who cares?"

We are creeping silently into the tunnel. I am holding my breath and it's not until we are a good twenty feet away that I let it out in a gust. "That was too close."

"I know," she says. Even in this light I can see she is pale from the scare. But then she grins. "But you have the phone and you know the code and that's what matters."

"Yeah," I say, the knowledge warm inside me.

I can't believe I didn't think of it before. Though of course to know that my dad chose the day he met me as his code, I'd have to know that he loved me and that I only fully realized an hour ago.

"I need to get back," Sera says. "I think you should still stock the weapons after you call, just in case we want to distract the agents when the police are breaking in or something."

"I'll do it as soon as I call."

Sera turns to me and smiles. "See you outside."

Without thinking I hug her. It's so familiar yet new somehow too. "Thanks."

She looks at me for a moment and I know she gets it. That's the thing I somehow let myself forget these past months: Sera always has my back and she always, always gets me.

CHAPTER 25

Sera

I am running as fast as I quietly can through the tunnels. I've been gone for ages and drawing air into my lungs is nearly impossible every time I think about what will be waiting for me when I get back. I take the stairs two at a time, trying not to think about it. It's hard enough to breathe in these musty tunnels.

I know I should be feeling relief about the phone but so much has gone wrong tonight that it's hard to feel secure about anything. Plus what if it takes them a while to get here? We're on a pretty tight deadline. At this point I think we need to carry on with our plans and hope the police are there as backup. I know Ariel will get the weapons there and Hudson can get them if I'm—okay, not thinking about that.

Instead I think about Ariel, how good it felt to talk to her, to tell her I'm not sorry and for her to get that. The absolute worst thing about these past nine months and four days wasn't the social freeze out or the death of my social life. It was losing my best friend.

I slow as I near the bathroom, then pause for a second to catch my breath. I still can't believe John Avery is behind all this. I mean, I can, the evidence is there, and given how much Mr. Barett yelled at him, I can see why he might not feel that loyal to him. Still, this is pretty extreme. And my heart aches for Ariel, though at least she knows her uncle didn't do it. Hard to know which is worse really—either way someone she trusted backstabbed her pretty harshly and that sucks.

I peer through the grate and see that no one is in the bathroom. I remove the grate as noiselessly as I can, slip back into the bathroom and put the grate back. Is it possible that the agents lost track of how long I've been in here? My hopes lift. They're tired and distracted and maybe the one who gave me permission to use the bathroom left. Maybe I really am going to get away with this.

I open the bathroom door and they are there, waiting for me. One grabs my arm so hard I squeal and the other is in my face yelling, "Where the hell were you?"

Behind them I can see my classmates and Hudson on the sofas. They look almost as terrified as I feel.

"Answer me!" he yells.

"The bathroom," I whisper.

"We'll deal with her upstairs," the other agent says, jerking my arm so brutally my eyes tear and I'm worried he's going to dislocate my shoulder. He shoves me toward the door.

Through blurry eyes I twist my head back and find Hudson's face.

"Brush-busting is set," I call out to him, hoping he'll understand that they need to go ahead with the plan. I am pushed out of the room before I can see his reaction.

They force me up the stairs so fast I trip and the tug on my arm to get me upright practically has me seeing stars. I struggle up, my mind back in the game room with my friends. I will not get to see what happens next, I know that. But I made sure they'd have the weapons and maybe I even helped Ariel call the police. It's possible they'll get here in time to save everyone, though not me. My window is closing too fast.

My face is wet with tears, my arm is screaming in pain, and fear is a thick fog in my belly. But my heart isn't back in that room with Hudson and Cassidy, it's in the tunnels with Ariel.

And it's my heart that matters.

CHAPTER 26

Ariel

I tap the phone to life but even as it lights up, it is flashing, telling me I have no power and it is going to shut down. It's possible I could at least dial 911 in this last millisecond except for one thing: There is no reception deep in the tunnels.

I can't get us help but maybe I can do one thing before the phone dies. I whip out the party plan and take a shot of the page that says John is in charge of security. That way if something happens to me and the actual pages, there is some proof that he is behind it. The phone shuts down, its light dying out. I take a moment to hide the plan in a corner, just in case I get caught, just to have another way someone might be able to figure out John is behind this, and then I head off to deliver the weapons.

It takes me three trips to get all the weapons in place and sweat is beaded at my temples by the time I am done. I am pleased with the stash though—there are more than enough weapons for everyone.

I head back upstairs and try to find Nico. It takes me a few minutes but I finally track him down in the hall outside my bedroom. I listen for a few moments but hear no other voices and take the risk.

"Nico," I whisper.

He starts, then whispers back. "Your room in three minutes."

I head to my room and wait just inside the grate until I hear him come in. His face is flushed and sweaty, and his hair is sticking up all over the place. These things should not make my stomach explode with fizzy, sweet bubbles like a shaken can of soda that send tingles across my body but they do and I take a second to get a grip, to mash down the fizz. Then I step out, my face neutral.

"I got the weapons downstairs," I tell him. "They're all set.

"Great," he says, wiping a hand across his forehead and smiling. He has such a nice smile. "Those of us on the inside are ready as well. When we hear the attack downstairs we will do our part."

"Good," I say, starting to pace. It's impossible to stand still with all the adrenaline I have coursing through me and it helps control the tingles I get when I look straight at him. Less than fifteen minutes now. "You guys should be sure to take off your ski masks, so no one thinks you're with the other agents."

He nods, probably having already thought of this.

"Do you think your uncle will try to escape?" Nico asks.

"Oh, I found out it wasn't him."

"No?" he asks. "How did you discover this?"

"They shot him."

His eyes fill with pain for me but instead of hardening me, like it should, it makes my insides go a little melty.

"I'm sorry," he says softly. Then he shakes his head. "I've said that a lot tonight."

"I guess a lot has happened," I say, trying to sound flippant but not even coming close.

Nico rubs his fingers down my cheek so gently it makes the fizzing bubbles go wild. "It has."

I step away before I do something stupid, something I will later regret. "I think John Avery is behind it." The words come out all choked, like my throat is constricting. I still can't believe John is behind this.

Nico's mouth presses into a line. "You know, that makes sense. I have seen him tonight, and his assistant, and they did not look scared like everyone else."

Right, Owen was here. That should have tipped me off.

"I guess they think they have nothing to fear," I say ruefully.

Nico grins at me. "So they think. They don't know that the lioness of God is onto them."

Somehow the really cheesy meaning of my name does not sound cheesy when he says it. And I remember what his name means, victory of the people. I realize it fits him. "There's a lot they don't know," I say.

I can't tear my eyes away from him, with his hair that sticks up straight, his rough features, his thick fingers able to create such beauty with the flowers he grows.

His brow wrinkles. "Wait, what will you do when the fighting starts?"

"I'll go downstairs," I say, having already thought it through. "I thought I'd jump out of the fireplace right after they start, just to give the agents something else they aren't expecting."

Nico nods. "It's a good idea." He glances at the clock. "I should go now."

"Wait." There's one part of my plan I haven't told him and don't intend to. But I need him to do something for me. "Can you hold onto this?" I reach into my pocket for the phone and hand it to him. "I took a picture of something that might help implicate John Avery as the person behind this whole thing. Can you keep it safe for me?"

He does not reach for it but instead just looks at me steadily. "You plan to confront John?" he asks after a moment.

So much for not telling him the other part of my plan. "I have to. But I'm not sure how it will go and if anything happens to me, I just want to know you have this and you'll give it to the police."

Now he reaches out his hand, but instead of taking the phone, he wraps his fingers around mine and the bubbles fizz up.

We hear voices in the hall and we both freeze.

"So where did she go if she wasn't in the bathroom?" an agent is saying as they come closer.

Nico stuffs the phone in his pocket and waves me toward the grate but I stay where I am, waiting to hear the response, my body suddenly going cold.

"No one knows," the other agent, a woman, replies. "But we checked every inch of that bathroom and she was gone. Then like fifteen minutes later she came out the door."

My whole body is ice.

"That's not really . . ." The voices fade as they turn the corner.

"What are you waiting for?" Nico whispers urgently. "They could come back. You must go."

"Sera," I manage to croak through my frozen lips. "They have Sera."

Nico's face suddenly looks like he has aged twenty years in the half-second it takes him to process what I've said. "You're sure?"

I nod.

"I will go see if there's anything I can do."

But I am already heading for the grate. It is my fault she was caught and I am going to be the one to fix this.

CHAPTER 27

Sera

The agents hustle me through the door of a small sitting room in Mr. Barett's office suite, which I am surprised to see is empty, save for a couple chairs and an empty desk. They shove me down in a high-backed armchair that is unpleasantly firm. Then they just stand there, like they're waiting for something. I am wondering if I should say something or if that would just make things worse. Since I don't have anything to say, I decide to stay quiet despite the fact that the silence is starting to feel noxious every time I breathe it in.

Then the door opens and The Assassin strides in. My heart lurches painfully in my chest. How could I have felt like the silence was a bad thing? I'd do anything to keep it longer.

"So it seems you have some secrets you'd like to share with us," The Assassin says.

My limbs feel tingly but in an awful way, like bugs are crawling on me. This is going to be the part where they threaten me, maybe even hurt me, to get me to tell them what I know. Whenever Ariel and I watched movies with torture scenes we'd talk about how we'd never give up our friends, even if we were being sliced up with machetes. But secretly I always wondered if I'd spill everything the second the machete came out of its sheath and now I realize I'm going to get the chance to find out.

"Not really, sir," I say, hoping manners help.

He smacks me across the face, hard. My neck snaps back and my cheek is on fire. I gasp and raise my hand to my injured face. I had no idea that being slapped hurt so much.

"Let's try that again," The Assassin says, his hand raised in case I'm too stupid to know what he'll do if he doesn't like my answer.

"Okay, that's enough of that," a familiar voice says.

At first I can't see him because my chair is facing away but he comes and stands in front of me, his salt and pepper hair perfectly combed as always, his suit neat despite the tension of the moment. But that is all that is the same about John Avery. His face, usually a mask of pleasant acquiescence, is sharp, his eyes cold as he looks me over.

"We don't need to get rough with Sera," he tells The Assassin. "She'll respond just fine to a reasonable conversation."

I so don't like the sound of that. Back in the tunnel I was feeling calm and accepting of things but now I feel like I am about to crawl out of my skin. My need to be out of this room and away from these people is a howl rising up inside me.

"Sera, I know you haven't been close to your classmates lately," John says, leaning back comfortably on the edge of the desk behind him. "But I feel certain you would not want to watch while we sliced off their fingers and cut their throats an inch at a time until they bled to death in front of you."

I think I am going to throw up. I can't believe this is John talking, the man who ordered pizza for us on sleepovers and stepped in for Ariel's dad at the last parent/student dinner we had. This man is not that genial father figure, this man is a psychopath.

"And I believe you have become friends with the singer," John says. "We can arrange for him to be first. Perhaps in his case it is his tongue we will cut out first."

I am choking on the bile that has risen in my throat, my body convulsing with each shattering cough. Through my teary eyes I see John nod, pleased with my reaction.

"There's something you'd like to tell us, isn't there," he says gently.

What can I do? How do I choose whose death warrant to sign? And how will I live with myself after I've chosen? Though that probably won't be a problem for long. John has revealed himself to me, there is no way I am walking out of this room alive.

"So tell us," John says, leaning down so his face is close to mine, his sour breath hot on my cheek. "How did you get out of the bathroom?"

I have to tell him something and in the tiny part of my brain that has managed to stay rational I realize that it comes down to numbers and odds. Maybe Ariel can still find a way to escape or maybe they won't find her right away and the attack will happen downstairs and she can join in. Or maybe the police will come. Ariel will have a shot, albeit a long shot, and that is better than the chances of all my classmates if they are led up here, tortured, and executed. So I clear my throat, which is raw and burning from the acidic bile.

"There are tunnels in the walls."

"What?" John asks, his eyes narrowing.

"It's from the Underground Railroad or something," I explain, my voice high and unfamiliar in my ears. "There are these tunnels inside the walls."

"How do you get into them?" he asks, looking at me closely to see if I am making the whole thing up.

"The metal grates, like the one in the fireplace in the living room," I say. Each word hurts. "They have little latches on them."

John considers this for a moment, then nods and smoothes his tie, like he has just completed a satisfying business transaction. "That would explain how she's managed to hide from us this long. And she is still there?"

It's too hard to answer that one so I just nod my head once.

"Let's go get her," John says to The Assassin and the other agents behind me.

He casts one last, reptilian smile at me. "Don't worry, we'll be back. And in case you wondered, there is nothing that can be used as a weapon in this room. We made sure of that before our first guest came."

He means Marc and the bile is back in the soft tissue of my throat, scalding and sharp.

Then they are gone, the door locked behind them. I sink down in the chair and let the tears come. I am a quivering pathetic mess. I sold out my best friend before they even got the machete out of the sheath. Yes, it was an impossible choice but there had to be something else I could have done. Or I should have at least dragged it out longer, given the police more time to get here, or stalled until after the attack started downstairs. Instead I caved in seconds because I was scared. Am scared. The thought of The Assassin's return has me in a blind panic. I don't want to be hurt and I don't want to die. I'm like a trapped animal, with nothing to defend me, nothing I can do to save myself. My stomach heaves in a final kind of way. I make it to the garbage can in time for the gush of puke that empties every last bit of my stomach contents out. Then I sit back in the chair, spent.

My body feels like a wrung-out towel but slowly I collect myself and realize that I am facing another choice. I can sit back and wait to be slaughtered or I can try and save myself. And obviously that's what I'm going to do. I'm not just going to sit here and wait for them to kill me. There has to be *something* I can do to fight back and maybe even escape. But first things first. My face is a mess of sweat and puke so I reach into my pocket for a tissue.

And that's when my fingers find the Swiss Army knife.

CHAPTER 28

Ariel

I am racing down the hall of the tunnel toward the upstairs game room, the spot closest to the office suite, when I hear something, something too close. I stop where I am and listen, a cold sweat prickling my face and sides, because the sound I hear is a grate opening. They know about the tunnels and this can only mean one thing: Sera told them. The sweat begins to snake down my sides. I don't want to know what they did or threatened her with to get her to tell, I just want to get to her as fast as I can, before anything else can happen. But now my best route is a no go.

I spin around and head for the back guest bedroom. It's not an ideal spot because I'll have to walk down two halls to reach the office suite, but it's close and who knows how many agents are going to start pouring into the tunnels. Hopefully enough to leave the halls somewhat empty.

I am getting close when I hear footsteps behind me. I gauge the distance but there is no way I can outrun this agent, open the grate in the guest bedroom, and get away. He is moving too fast for that. So I stop and turn, ready to fight with everything I've got. I know the agents are trained killers or whatever but honestly, the way I am feeling right now, this guy is going to be lucky to make it out of here in one piece. I am poised, hands in front of me ready to claw his eyes, when he suddenly stops.

"Ariel?" he breathes.

"Rock star?" I ask in disbelief, lowering my hands.

"I'm glad I found you," he says. "These tunnels are like a maze and I am so lost."

"What are you doing in them?"

"Sera," he says, his voice breaking the tiniest bit. "They took Sera and I'm trying to find her."

Wow, Sera really made an impression on this guy who is so not just any guy.

"I'm trying to find her too," I say. "My guess is they have her in one of the rooms in the office suite."

"So let's go," he says.

I start walking, talking as we go. "The only problem is that the office suite is a new addition so there aren't any tunnel entrances into any of the rooms. I was heading to one of the closer spots but we'll have to walk through the halls to get there."

"Okay," he says, walking so fast he steps on the heel of my sneaker. He doesn't apologize and I speed up, ears pricked in case any agents in the tunnels come close.

The guest room is dark and the grate swings open noiselessly. So far so good. We step out quietly and walk to the doorway. I peek around and then snap my head back fast because two agents are in the hall about ten feet away, in the direction we need to go, and they are hanging out, chatting.

"Getting tired . . ." one of the agents says.

"I know," the other one says. "Just standing around all night is boring."

"Tell me about it," the first one says. "I thought we'd see a little action but up here it's just pacing and watching the office guys go by."

Hudson and I back into the room. "Let's get back to the tunnels and come out somewhere else," he whispers.

I shake my head. "They know about the tunnels. It's not safe in there anymore."

"Wait, how did they find out?"

I clear my throat but don't actually speak. I'm afraid if I say Sera's name I might lose it.

But it doesn't take long for Hudson to get it. He draws in a sharp breath. "We have to get to her," he says. In the dim light from the hall I can see him running his hand through his hair.

"Yeah, I know," I say. "So this is what I think we do. You go out there and get the agents to follow you away from the offices. Then I can sneak to the suite and help Sera."

"Not to sound like I just crawled out of a cave but I'm a lot bigger than you are and I think I have a better shot of getting her out of there," he says.

I am truly going soft because rather than annoying me I actually find his chivalry slightly endearing.

"If there are ten guards out there with guns, then neither of us is going to be able to get her out," I say. "But it's me they want. If I show up that will take the heat off Sera."

"Wait, so I'm supposed to just let you walk out there and sacrifice yourself?" he asks. "I don't think so."

He really did just crawl out of a cave, though a very gallant one.

"It's just what makes the most sense," I say, resting what I hope is a soothing hand on his arm to pacify him and also to get him to do what I need him to do. "I have the element of surprise on my side too. Plus, once you ditch those two agents you can come in and then we'll have another surprise working for us."

He sighs. "I guess you're right but I go on record as not liking this."

I would laugh if I had it in me. "Duly noted."

"So where is the office suite after I get rid of these guys?" he asks.

"Right to the end of this hall, then turn left." I tell him. I don't want to think about how slim the chances are that he will actually get there, but then none of us has good odds here. "I'm not sure which room she'll be in. There's the main office plus three other rooms and a bathroom."

"I'll find you guys," he says.

I expect him to talk for a bit about his plan for the agents in the hall but he just strides out, grabbing a vase off the bedside table as he goes. In the square of light from the doorway I see him hurl the vase, then take off in the opposite direction from the suite. I hear a crash, a howl, and then two figures in army green are streaking after him.

This is it. I sneak out into the hall that is now empty and race as quietly as I can to the end of the hall, then peek around to the left. Two agents are walking toward me. I leap into the nearest room, a TV room, and wait behind the door, heart thudding in my throat, hoping they didn't see me.

"I can't believe how far this has gone," one of them, a woman, says. "I never signed on to kill a bunch of kids."

They have stopped near the doorway and I grit my teeth, hoping they will move on.

"Yeah, me neither," the guy says. "But then it's not like we have to shoot them point blank. We're just setting the place on fire."

Why aren't they moving? I want to scream in frustration and their stupid conversation is doing nothing to calm me down.

But then I hear a rustling, as though they are straightening up.

"Hello Mr. Avery," the first guy says, his voice deferential.

"Good evening," John says, his voice and nearness making my insides curdle. "I trust everything is going smoothly over here?"

"Absolutely," the second agent says.

"I'm glad to hear it," John says, in the same voice that read me *Paddington Bear*. "We just have one final piece of business and then we'll begin wrapping things up. You can head downstairs at that point."

The words pierce me, like a sharp blade slicing deep. That last piece of business is Sera, and her they will shoot point blank.

"Carry on," John says, heading down the hall, his footsteps growing fainter.

I can't wait this out anymore, not when John is going in that room to kill Sera. So I take a page from Hudson's book and grab the lamp off the end table, almost tripping over the cord. I hoist it over my head like a football and run out into the hall.

CHAPTER 29

Sera

I am crawling out of my skin by the time the door finally opens ten minutes later. The knife is still in my pocket. It's too small to use to rush at someone from a distance, it's more the kind of thing you use up close, like when someone's trying to kill you. So it's stowed in my pocket, comforting and cool against my hip.

The Assassin comes in, followed by John Avery.

"The transfer is complete and the plane is ready to go at the airport," John says to The Assassin. "It will take us about fifteen minutes to get there."

Fifteen minutes to the airport means they are taking the helicopter to the small airport for private planes. By the time it's discovered that Mr. Barett is dead and everyone at the party has been killed, they will be long gone.

"And we have the gasoline ready for the fire," John continues. "We should have Ariel any minute so that will be taken care of as well. Are there people assigned to the doors?"

"Yes, that's been taken care of," The Assassin says. "They'll get started downstairs locking up the windows and doors in about twenty minutes, and then the only escape will be the roof."

My insides are a tangled mess. First, this sounds grisly and awful and I realize that it's not just my classmates being killed, it's a bunch of agents too, the ones who know too much or are just expendable. But second, the thing cutting into me like a dull razor, is the fact that they are talking about this in front of me. Which has to mean that they are close to killing me.

"I think we're set then," John says, smoothing his tie. "Just take care of her and then you can follow up downstairs."

Panic is clawing its way up my throat as The Assassin turns to me, casually reaching for his gun.

The door bursts open.

"Stop!" someone shouts. Someone tall and blond and really, really angry.

I have never been so glad to see Ariel.

Unfortunately two more agents run in after, one who seems to have bits of glass in his hair. In chaos, the agents try to grab Ariel. Ariel slips away, rushing over and throwing her arms around me. That's when I close my eyes, sinking into her, the smell of French lavender suddenly the most amazing smell in the world. Around me I hear shouts, a chair falling over, footsteps, but in this moment, leaning on Ariel's shoulder, I feel safe.

"I'd like everyone to shut the hell up."

My eyes snap open, the security ripped away like a blanket being torn off me. It's John Avery speaking, whose face is red, whose eyes are burning, and who is looking right at Ariel. The agents go silent but Ariel glares back at John. She lets go of me and puts her hands on her hips. I sink back against the desk, my legs shaking too hard to hold me up.

"How could you?" Ariel's voice is strong 'til the last word when it cracks just the tiniest bit.

John hears it, I can tell by the way his posture softens. "It's business," he says. "And you have made it much harder than it should have been."

"It's not business, you killed my dad!" Ariel shouts. "That's about as personal as it gets."

John's face is blank. "He deserved it."

"What about me?" Ariel asks. Her hair is coming loose and tendrils fall over her forehead. "Do I deserve it too?"

John looks away, which kind of surprises me. Or maybe it doesn't, I don't know. But it has to mean something to Ariel that he does obviously have some genuine feelings for her.

"And it's not the first time, is it?" Ariel asks. "You were the one who planned Mexico, weren't you?"

John sighs. "What does it matter now?"

"I want to know," Ariel says, impatiently brushing her hair off her face. "You can at least give me that since you killed my dad."

John rests a hand on the back of the chair he's standing next to. "Yes, I planned Mexico," he says. "It was a much simpler operation but there was a snitch at the last minute and the police got there before we could finish."

"Would you have had me killed then?" Ariel asks, her voice ragged at the edges.

John doesn't answer.

"You would have had to, right, since I'm the one who's going to inherit the company?" she asks.

I draw in a breath at this news but John actually squeezes the back of the chair as though he would collapse if he weren't gripping it.

"How did you know?" he asks. "I've had every copy of that will destroyed."

"And destroyed the lawyer who made it too, right?"

John is clearly taken aback by all Ariel has figured out. The corner of Ariel's mouth turns up but her face is too cold for it to be a smile.

"My dad made sure I knew," she tells him.

"He said he wasn't going to reveal his choice to you until you graduated college," John says, his cheeks losing their pink.

"I guess you don't know everything about him," Ariel says.

John steeples his fingers for a moment. "It doesn't really make any difference now."

A thick silence hangs in the room for a moment. It's the closest he's come to saying he plans to have Ariel killed and from the way she recoils just slightly, I see that she hears it too. But then she pulls her shoulders back and stands even straighter.

"After Mexico my dad got more security," she says.

John nods.

"So you had to work harder to come up with a plan," she prompts.

John loosens his grip on the chair but his face is pale. "Yes, he was suspicious of everyone after that. I wasn't sure I would get another opportunity, but then he put me in charge of security for the party. I knew it would be my last shot. And a good one with all the extra hostages."

"So you did it right," she says bitingly. "Hiring a bunch of sadistic mercenaries who were happy to kill unarmed kids."

The Assassin shifts, clearly not in love with that description of himself. "Are we done listening to this?"

John starts to speak but Ariel interrupts him. "It was the perfect plan except for one thing."

This time John looks right at her. "What would that one thing be?"

"There's proof that you were the one who was in charge of security," she says. "When the police find that they'll start a manhunt for you."

I expect John to be angry but instead he actually smiles. "I find that unlikely. But even if you did have some kind of evidence it will burn when the house burns."

"It's not on paper," Ariel says. "It's on a phone. And it won't be in the house when it burns."

"That's not possible," The Assassin says quickly. It's funny how his voice is different around John Avery, nervous and almost timid. Which is actually pretty scary. "We collected every phone."

"Except for my father's," Ariel says. "That one you never found."

John turns to The Assassin, his eyes now serpentine, and once again I see the man capable of killing all these people.

"Is this true?" he hisses.

"We were going to tell you," The Assassin says. "But we figured it just got thrown out with the body."

Ariel winces at that.

"You figured wrong it seems," John snarls. He has become something feral.

"I—" The Assassin begins.

"Go find it and bring it to me," John snaps.

"Okay," The Assassin says, moving toward the door.

"Good luck," Ariel singsongs. It's like poking a caged tiger but there's nothing he can do besides glare at her on his way out.

"Where is it?" John asks Ariel.

"Like I'm going to tell you," she scoffs.

"I'm not asking again," he says, his voice deadly.

Ariel leans forward, her face close to his. "Go to hell."

John steps back, his face now red, his eyes lit from a flame within. "Kill them immediately."

The first agent grabs Ariel while the other starts for me. But just then the door to the room flies open. I think it will be The Assassin or other agents ready to shoot us, so it is a complete shock to see that the person in the doorway is Hudson. His hair is sticking up straight like he's been running his hands through it, his cheeks are pink, and he is panting, as though he has been running. He is also brandishing my bottle of hair spray. He takes stock of things, of John in front of him, the agents frozen in attack position, me and Ariel cowering—and he starts fighting.

He gets John right in the face with the hair spray, which must sting because John goes down with a howl of pain, his hands over his face. Next is the agent after Ariel whom Hudson sprays and then kicks in the knee. The agent staggers backwards, clawing at his eyes. Last is the agent after me who throws a punch that hits Hudson in the jaw. I wince but Hudson doesn't miss a beat as he sprays him in the eyes, then punches back, hard enough that the guy staggers backwards and trips over the desk, his hands scrubbing at his face, his elbow knocking the bottle out of Hudson's hands.

"Run!" Hudson shouts, racing for the door.

But standing there in the doorway is The Assassin.

For a moment we all freeze as he pulls out his gun. I see the defeat on Hudson's face, see Ariel slump. But this is not over yet. I lunge forward, the Swiss Army knife in my hands, my fingers pulling out the blade so that it is sharp and ready. I stab it deep into his chest, the slick sound of slicing flesh and popping tendons nauseating. But I don't stop until the blade is buried in him.

Blood spurts from the wound and he staggers back, screaming in pain.

Hudson grabs my arm. I grab Ariel and we fly down the hall, toward the stairs. A group of agents at the top of the staircase start toward us but then we hear it, the yelling from downstairs.

Our attack has started.

CHAPTER 30

Ariel

The scene in the game room is sheer pandemonium. A crowd clusters around the bathroom but just as we get there Aisha flies out and someone slams the door behind her. Ravi is right there with a folding chair that he wedges under the door knob, effectively locking it from the outside. A loud cheer arises from my classmates and I hear pounding on the door.

The agents in the room are up and trying to get their guns but Cassidy's group is ready, mostly attacking from behind with heavy objects, like bookends, though I see a stiletto heel raised high. I did well choosing the weapons. More agents are coming in but Franz gives a signal to a group of four students who are waiting by the doorways and as soon as the agents walk in they are sprayed in the face, then tackled to the floor in that moment of weakness. Some agents make it through and a group led by Ella is there to meet them.

The room is a cloud of hair products and scuffling sounds and yelling. It's funny, no one has even noticed I'm here. They're all too focused on the task at hand. I see Ravi wrestling with an agent who towers over him and they both go down. Ella is backed into a corner by two agents but Lulu comes behind them with a can of shaving cream and her aim is true. The agents are blinded by the cream and Lulu and Ella run. I grin. That was just what I was thinking when I put the shaving cream in the stash of weapons.

Then I hear it, the first shot, followed by screams. In the far corner of the room, near the stage that was set up for Hudson's concert, an agent has a gun and someone goes down. Instinctively I start over, to see if there's anything I can do to help but Hudson grabs my arm.

"We need to start clearing the escape route," he yells to me over the chaos of the room.

He's right, that's the most important thing to do right now.

We start for the doorway to the living room, Sera is with us, but in front of us is an agent pulling out his gun. I'm closest so I waste no time rushing over to kick him in the back of the knee, hard. The solidity of his flesh hurts my foot so much I cry out but he's the one in real pain, going down in a crumple. I wrestle his gun out of his hands, not sure I can actually do anything with it. I could see myself accidently shooting one of my classmates. But better for me to have it than him.

I turn around and come face to face with Cassidy who is staring at me, eyes wide like she's seeing a ghost. I stiffen, ready for her to yell at me, but instead she just raises an eyebrow muttering something about a weapons source.

"Your makeup is a mess," she tells me.

I laugh but then more shots ring out across the room, followed by shrieks and someone's gut-wrenching wail.

"I've got that," Cassidy says, taking the gun out of my hands with a practiced manner. She lifts the gun comfortably. "Looks like all those hours at the shooting range are about to pay off," she says, closing one eye and taking aim at an agent who has his own gun raised.

"Shoot to maim, not kill," Hudson says.

"I'm making sure no one can shoot back," Cassidy snaps as Franz charges an agent with a letter opener a few feet away.

She fires and sure enough the agent, who was hit in the shoulder of his shooting arm, goes down hard.

"Grab his gun!" Cassidy yells to Ravi and Ella who are standing closest to the fallen agent.

"You're a good shot," Hudson tells Cassidy.

"I know," she says, taking aim at another armed agent. "Go clear the escape route already."

Hudson, Sera, and I head for the door. The air is still thick with hair products but it's underlined with the smoky salt of gunpowder and the metallic smell I can now identify as blood. An agent runs into the room and Carson, the star linebacker, charges him, a large picture frame held high, which he smashes over the agent's head. I jump back to avoid being hit by debris.

"Nice one," I tell him.

He does a double take when he sees me, then grins. "Yeah, I've never been big on art."

I catch up with Hudson and Sera who are at the doorway to the living room, which appears empty. Of course it makes sense that any agents would have come in here by now. The challenge will be getting to the front door.

I can't help glancing back toward the doorway near the staircase but there is no sign of Nico. I wonder how they are faring upstairs but there's no time to dwell on it, not now.

"Okay, Hudson and I will clear the way," I say over the sound of more gunfire. "Sera, make sure none of the agents sneak up behind us and then start getting everyone to follow."

She nods, wincing at the sound of a nearby bullet.

"Let's go," Hudson says.

We head into the living room and he goes straight to the fireplace and grabs a poker for each of us.

"These look like medieval weapons," I say, liking the heft of mine in my hands. This could really do damage.

More shots come from the living room and we head to the doorway, then look out into the foyer. Behind us I hear people coming out of the living room, following Sera.

"It looks good," Hudson says, but just then two agents run down the big staircase.

We duck back in, hiding on either side of the wide doorway.

"You ready?" Hudson asks.

Dumb question and I just roll my eyes. I've been itching to take some of these people down since the second this whole thing started. I lift my poker and when the first agent comes through I bring it sailing down, right across his belly.

He gasps and I realize he is a she. She clutches her middle and falls on the floor, tripping the agent coming in behind her.

"Come on!" Hudson shouts to everyone, shoving the agents aside and racing for the front door.

I hear shouting from the stairs and see two agents racing down, followed by two more with their ski masks off, and my heart leaps in my chest because one of them is Nico. The first agent has a gun and lifts it, but Cassidy takes him out with one shot. That girl is *good*. The second agent pauses, giving just enough time for Nico's friend to whack him on the head with a heavy crystal vase. He goes down in a heap.

Everyone is now rushing to get to the front door and my eyes are watering from the hair products and gunpowder that have formed a misty cloud in the air. People are shouting, agents are trying to pull people back, but someone, probably Hudson, wrenches the front door open and people begin to pour outside. I see Sera catch up with Hudson and they duck out into the early morning light together.

But I wait for Nico and feel delicious tingles when his eyes find me and his whole face lights up.

"You're okay," he says, coming over and resting one of his callused hands gently on my cheek. And in the midst of the shooting and yelling and smoky air the bubbles are fizzing away inside me, exquisite and sweet.

"You are too," I say stupidly.

He suddenly looks up and I turn to see three agents running toward us.

"Shut the door!" one of them shouts.

Franz comes up behind them armed with a golf club but as soon as he hits one of them, the other two turn on him.

Nico and I race over and Ella comes from the other direction. I smack down one of the guys with my poker but the other one has his gun out and Nico grabs his arm just as he shoots. The first bullet flies away harmlessly but the second hits Ella right between the eyes.

I think her death is instant because her eyes don't even close. She just sinks down as blood spews from the hole in her head.

Franz's hands cover his mouth as he steps back in horror. Nico has managed to wrestle the agent to the ground and I stamp on his wrist with all my strength, then grab his gun when he shrieks and lets go of it. I'd shoot his head off if I knew how.

Nico sees my face and stands up quickly, taking the gun from me.

"Kill him," I say hoarsely, not even sure if Nico knows anything about guns. But then the way he clicks the safety into place and settles it under his arm tells me that he knows exactly how to shoot to kill. "What are you waiting for?" I ask, a hysterical edge to my voice.

Ella is bleeding all over my shoes and the iron smell of it is clogging my throat.

"Revenge doesn't change anything," he says. "Believe me, I know."

"That's bull," I say, but I allow him to take my arm and to lead me and a stricken Franz to the front door. We look out onto the endless grassy expanse of my front yard and stop short.

Despair slithers up from my belly to my chest as I take in the scene of agents lined up in the driveway, shooting my classmates like they are fish in a barrel. My classmates are yelling, hiding, trying to stem blood flowing from the ones that are wounded. And those are the lucky ones. I can't bear to look at the bodies lying on the grass, unmoving.

We made it this far but this is obviously the end of the road. There's no way we're going to get past these guys. It's over.

So I do the only thing I can in what are probably the last few minutes of my life. I take Nico's face in my hands and I kiss him.

CHAPTER 31

Sera

Hudson and I are the first ones out of the house and when we see all the agents in the yard, so many more than we had realized, we stop. But people are swarming, pushing out around us so we move forward with the momentum.

"We have to do something, create some kind of distraction," Hudson says to me over the din.

He's right but it's hard to think, especially since I've been trying to shut my mind off this whole time. I am haunted by the feeling of the knife going into The Assassin, his scream as he fell, the blood pouring out of the wound, the wound that I made. I know I have to do something, just like I know Cassidy has to be shooting agents and my other classmates have to be taking them down any way they can; that's what us against them means. But I just can't stomach how horrible it feels to hurt another person.

"What about the garage?" Hudson asks, looking toward the big white structure next to the house.

I do what I can to shove all thoughts of The Assassin to a dark corner of my mind. The garage is a great idea. And even better, there's no one to hurt there.

"This way," I tell Hudson, as the surprised outdoor agents start pulling out their guns.

No one notices as we race along the short stone path to the garage, probably because it's mostly blocked off from the front yard by weeping willow trees. The garage is locked but this code I know, or at least I knew, so I cross my fingers and press in five numbers. There is a click and the side door opens and we walk in. For a moment we are in darkness and then I flick on the light.

"Awesome," Hudson breathes as he looks over the ten-car garage. It is cleaner than many homes, with slick white walls, the smooth floor glistening with shiny black paint, and a large silver metal shelving unit filled with car parts and fluids. The big lights overhead create an almost museum effect casting a bright glow over Mr. Barett's one leisure activity: seven gleaming sports cars.

Hudson walks carefully, as though on hallowed ground as he approaches the first one, resting his hand gently on the hood. "No way, this can't be an actual 1963 Porsche 911."

I can't believe he's having a boy moment *now*. "So we could hang out here and drool over these cars or use them to help us escape," I say, folding my arms across my chest.

Hudson looks back at me, appropriately sheepish. "Right, sorry," he says. Then he frowns. "I'm not sure we can just drive one of these out of here. They'd shoot out the tires before we got ten feet down the driveway."

"Yeah," I say, having already thought of that. "I think we'd be best off using them as a distraction, like driving them into the agents."

"Makes sense," he says. "If we could find bricks or something to put some pressure on the gas pedals we could get them all going nuts out there. That would probably be most effective."

Shots ring out outside and the ticking clock weighs heavily on me. I look around the garage for bricks but then see something else.

"What about these bottles of oil?" I ask.

"Let's give it a try."

His voice is taut and I know the shots have effected him the same way. I toss him a bottle and he gets into one of the cars, ducking out of sight to fit the bottle on the gas pedal. "It's not going to work," he says after a minute.

I hear screaming outside and I am starting to feel desperate. "Mr. Barett always left keys in the ignitions because the garage was locked. Can we just start them and push them out?" I ask. "It's on a hill so they could coast down. And we could drive the last two."

"Perfect," he says, starting the engine of one car. "Let's get three of them started, then open the door and push them out one after the other."

He starts up two other cars while I wait at the garage door opener. When he gives me a signal I press the button and the huge metal door slides up.

I rush over to Hudson and we push the first car. Needless to say it's really heavy and we are both heaving, my back aching, before we finally get it to start moving. But once it's in motion, it picks up speed on the hill and starts down the drive, toward what appears to be a line of agents shooting people. I see bodies on the ground and smell the gunpowder mixed with the crisp fall air, but I don't look to see who is down. We have more cars to get out there.

"This is brilliant," Ravi says, coming in the door of the garage, his face streaked with dried blood that must have come from someone else because he appears fine. He runs over and helps us push the second car. It's easier with three of us.

We hear less shooting now and when we get this car out the door I see that the agents are running or looking around trying to figure out what's going on, no longer just mowing down my classmates.

We rush back and get the next three cars moving. Two agents try to stop us but now my classmates are onto our plan and the agents are stopped with golf clubs and fire pokers before they reach us. A few people, including Franz, whose eyes are glassy and distant in a way that unsettles me, come in to help.

"Let's drive these last two," Ravi says, already settling into the driver's seat of the Porsche 911.

Franz lights up at this and jumps into the second car. He revs the engine and a moment later peels out of the garage, steering straight for a group of agents who all scatter. Ravi follows, less manic than Franz who is clearly trying to actually kill agents.

Hudson and I are just outside the main doorway of the garage, looking out at a changed scene. The cars have done their work. The agents are no longer a unified firing squad. Some still have their guns raised and are shooting but most of my classmates are either behind porch pillars or trees, out of range. The first five cars have already disappeared out of sight but Ravi and Franz are still wreaking havoc.

"We did it," I say, turning to Hudson.

And that's when I'm hit.

CHAPTER 32

Ariel

It's pretty much the best kiss of my life. Nico's lips are like velvet, his hands feather-soft on my face as he cradles it gently, like I am something precious. I have delicious shivers from head to toe and everything else slips away, the gunshots, the shouts, the chaos. It's just Nico's body pressed against mine.

And then a round of cheering goes up, so loud it can't be ignored. Nico and I break apart and I look around, my heart still pounding, and see my dad's black Ferrari FXX cruising slowly down the driveway, *sans* driver. It picks up speed as it goes and the agents who were standing there are now racing out of the way of the car.

Before they can regroup, another car, my dad's red Lamborghini Murcielago, is making its way down the drive.

"Sera," I say, not realizing I spoke out loud until Nico laughs.

"That was a really good idea," he says. "Let's get out of here and get help."

He's right, we need to go now while the cars are causing chaos and the agents are distracted. If we can get to the end of the driveway and wave down a car, or run to one of my neighbor's homes, we can call the police and finally, finally end this.

The only problem is there are still agents with guns and they are still shooting at us.

I turn to Nico who is holding the gun he got off the agent who killed Ella. "Maybe we should . . . "

He suddenly looks behind me, his eyes wide. He grabs me, throwing me down on the porch so hard I gasp. My knees and hands are raw and I look up in time to see the agent not ten feet away, his gun leveled, the bullet in the air. The bullet meant for me.

It hits Nico somewhere in his torso and he goes down hard, his body folded in half. His blood pools over my hands and knees at an alarming rate. I reach for him, feel that he is still warm, still alive. And then behind me I hear the gun cock a second time, this time for me.

I lunge forward, grabbing the gun that Nico dropped, the bullet whizzing over my head. My hands are sticky with blood but I manage to unlock the safety on the second try, remembering what Nico did to set it in the first place. Then I turn around and start shooting, not to take out but to kill.

CHAPTER 33

Sera

I am dying. I have to be because pain this bad can't mean anything else. There is a whooshing sound in my ears and my head feels like it's filled with cotton.

But instead of seeing a light or whatever happens when you die, I am being pulled behind a tree near the garage and Hudson is gently setting me down, then taking off his shirt.

I guess this could be heaven.

But then he starts to wrap the shirt around my shoulder, making me screech in pain.

"Hang in there, it's just a flesh wound," he says, tightening the shirt around my bleeding shoulder. To be honest it's not even that much blood but still, the pain is near blinding.

"How can you say *only*?" I manage to choke out.

"I've been there," he says. "When I was ten I was out hunting with my dad and my brother Tommy and I got grazed by a bullet, deeper than this actually. I was fine."

"Really, fine?" I ask. I'm kind of amazed I can be sarcastic in this moment, though the pain is ebbing a bit.

He grins. "I'm tough like that."

With the orange glow of the sunrise behind him it's hard to miss how perfect his chest is, how supple the muscles are when he reaches to help me up. I know there's something wrong with me to be thinking this right now so I look away, take his hand, and let him pull me up.

"I know it stings but honestly it barely took off much skin," he says. "You probably don't even need to go to the hospital."

"Are you calling me a wimp?" I ask.

He laughs. "Never." Then the lightness falls from his face and his grip on my hand tightens. "We have to go now."

I look at the scene in the yard, the agents still shooting, Ravi and Franz still driving around, my classmates hiding out as best they can, the ones who are not lying in the grass, that is. I look for Ariel but there are so many people crowded near the porch pillars and nearest trees that it's hard to find her. I don't want to stick my head out too far. One bullet wound is enough for today. And it is still really painful.

"Are you ready?" Hudson asks. "Because we have to do this now, while the cars are still a distraction. You and Ariel are the only ones who know the best way out of here and I'm not sure where she is, so it's got to be you." Then he squeezes my hand gently. "You and me."

I look away, so as not to get melty. But when I take a step forward I suddenly feel light-headed, and my knees buckle. He grabs me before I can fall and even in this state I feel shivers when he holds me against his chest.

"Are you okay?" he asks.

"Yeah, I don't know, I just feel really woozy," I say, closing my eyes for a minute. He lays me down on the ground. "I think it's the not eating and then the puking and now the whole getting shot thing." It's also the fact that I can't shake off the feeling of having stabbed The Assassin but I don't feel like talking about that.

He doesn't answer and when I open my eyes I see that he's gone. I lift myself up on one elbow and then I see him. He has crept over to the lilac bush next to the garage where he carefully snaps off a twig, then comes back over.

"These are your favorite, right?" he asks.

"Well, yeah, when there are actual flowers on them," I say to disguise how happy I am that he remembered such a small thing about me.

"Yeah, it would be better if this was spring and I could give you a real flower. But consider it a promise of future flowers. Future flowers that you can only get if you can get us out of here."

I reach out my hand and he hoists me up. Then he wraps my arm around his shoulders, being careful not to jar my injured one, so he can bear some of my weight. The feeling of him being so close is intoxicating.

"Okay, so where do we go?" he asks.

I consider for a moment. The backyard is something like half a mile long plus the woods at the back are really dense and hard to get through. Our best bet is to make it to the front gate and try and flag down a car there. If we go back behind the garage there is a ridge that would shield us a bit. We'd have to move fast but with most of my classmates bunched in front of the house, it's possible the agents won't even be looking that way.

"Behind the garage," I say. "And then—"

I stop midsentence and Hudson freezes at the exact same moment. I can feel his heart rate accelerate as my breath gets trapped in my lungs. Leaning out the window, his chest still dripping blood, is The Assassin. A gun rests in his arms, a gun he raises to point straight at us. There is no time to run and no place to run anyway. He is less than twenty feet away with nothing at all to block his shot.

We are sitting ducks.

As The Assassin releases the safety and takes aim, Hudson tries to move so that he's standing in front of me, blocking my body with his.

And then, just as I am preparing for another bullet to rip into me, my whole body steeled for the pain, The Assassin's head explodes. His brain splatters over the rose bushes, his blood soaking the grass. The gun falls from his still fingers.

I jerk backwards, wrenching my injured shoulder and crying out in pain. But it's good because pain means that I am still alive.

"We're okay," Hudson says, astonished. "Someone saved us."

I look toward the porch to see who had our backs and standing there is Ariel, gun steady in her hands. I start toward her but she shakes her head.

"Go!" she shouts.

And we do. We race around the back of the garage, then streak across the yard, partially hidden by the ridge. I hear gunshots but neither of us looks back. My head is pounding but Hudson is half-carrying me at this point and I put every ounce of my will into keeping upright, keeping my feet moving forward. It feels like time has stopped, like we are in this space of racing forever. There's just the ache in my chest from running, the uneven lawn beneath our feet, and Hudson's arm around me as the gunshots grow fainter.

Finally, we reach the gates and sprint through to the road beyond. A car is coming and Hudson lets go of me to step out in front of it, waving his hands like a madman.

The car slams on its brakes and pulls over to the side of the road. A woman sticks her head out the window.

"What's wrong with you?" she yells. "I could have killed you."

"Ma'am I apologize for startling you but we need the police, there's an emergency at the Barett home," Hudson says. "Could we trouble you to call 911?"

Her face softens at his charming Southern manners. "Of course," she says, picking up her phone. "What kind of emergency?"

"A hostage situation," Hudson says.

Already it doesn't even seem real, not here on this pretty stretch of highway, a Mercedes gliding by, the sun just coming up in the sky casting a golden glow over everything. You can barely smell the gunpowder here.

The woman looks at me, her eyes on the blood oozing the tiniest bit from my shoulder, and she punches in the numbers fast.

Hudson turns to me. "We did it."

I feel like we should be yelling or cheering but all I can do is look into his eyes, the eyes that have seen all the terrible events of the past twelve hours, the eyes that are now looking at me like I am more than just some flat-chested high school girl. A lot more.

He reaches out and tucks a stray lock of my hair behind my ear, then lets his fingers slide slowly down my cheek. Sparks crackle across my whole body as he leans down and kisses me, his lips deliciously soft against mine. I wrap my arms around him, pulling him closer as we kiss and kiss and kiss.

"They're on their way," the woman says, getting out of her car.

We break apart as she comes over. Despite the lack of sleep, the blood stains, and the way I probably smell, I know that I am glowing.

"Hey, aren't you Hudson Winters?" she asks.

"Actually," I say, grabbing his hand and lacing our fingers together as I hear the first sirens in the background. "It's Hunter."

CHAPTER 34

Ariel

"Are you sure you don't want me to wait?" Sera asks. We are standing at the top of the driveway near the porch steps. Hudson is a few feet away chatting with the driver of the car his manager sent over as soon as he heard about what happened.

Sera's shoulder has been wrapped by one of the paramedics and is now encased in neat white bandages. Her cheek has a streak of dirt, her clothes are sweat-stained, and her hair is falling out of its bun in loose tendrils. Despite all this her face is radiant and I have a feeling the reason for this is the same reason a horde of reporters and photographers are bunched just beyond the yellow tape at the end of the driveway. Hudson Winters.

"I'm sure," I tell her. "But thanks."

After the police arrived everything happened quickly. Most of the agents were quick to surrender and the few who didn't were taken out sniper-style. The paramedics took care of the injured, from splinting Cassidy's broken finger to strapping Ravi up on a body board. It's unlikely he will ever walk again but he is alive, which is more than Ella or Lulu can say. Some of us came away physically unscathed, like me and Carson, our injuries tucked away on the inside. Franz, whose eyes were vacant, could not stop biting at the skin around his fingernails, gnawing until they bled. Him they lead gently into the back of the ambulance, talking the whole time in soothing tones.

Now the police are doing a sweep of the house, going room to room to root out any hidden agents and to break into the office where John has barricaded himself. When they are done I will be allowed back into the house that was once my home.

"I don't want to leave you here alone," Sera says.

She looks out over the yard that is torn up from the cars. Ribbons of blood are spilled across it. The cars themselves are now crumples of metal, one wrapped around a tree after Ravi was shot and crashed into it, the other destroyed when Franz drove it into the side of the garage. I think he might have been trying to kill himself but he came out of it without a scratch on him. Piled neatly in the driveway, next to the ambulance, are the body bags.

"I know but I just, I think I need to be alone right now," I tell her. It's kind of hard to talk. My throat feels coated with syrup and words keep getting stuck there.

She sighs, then hugs me hard. "Okay, but you'll be over soon?"

The plan is for me to go to Sera's for the night, and maybe for the nights after too, until I figure out where to go. I'll certainly never spend another night here.

"Yeah," I say, trying to hug her back but not really managing. My body feels stiff, like it's not quite mine anymore.

Sera walks over to Hudson and when I see the glow on his face as he looks down at her, I have to turn away. I walk up the porch steps and sit on the top one, staring out as the car with Hudson and Sera in it winds down the drive, not really seeing it. Not really seeing anything.

"Ms. Barett?" a voice behind me says, startling me.

"Yes." I struggle to my feet because I can tell from his anxious expression that there is news.

"We got into the office suite and it seems that Mr. Avery has taken his own life." His voice is subdued, like this information will be less harsh to hear if it is delivered gently.

"I have to go up there," I tell him.

He recoils slightly, like I have said something inappropriate and maybe I have. Maybe there is something wrong with me for needing to see John Avery one last time, even if he is dead.

"That might not be such a good idea," another officer says, resting a comforting hand on my shoulder. "You did say you believed he was the one behind the hostage situation?"

I shake off his hand. "No, I said I *knew* he was the one behind the hostage situation," I say, thinking how absurdly civilized the term "hostage situation" is—it doesn't evoke panic and death and the smell of blood, it sounds more like a mishap with a seating chart at a dinner party. "And I do need to see John."

The cops exchange a look but I don't bother to wait and hear their decision, I just walk into the house. The smell inside the doorway, the residual gunpowder, the blood, and then the slightly sour scent that I know is terror still hovering in a thin mist stops me for a moment but then I keep going. The first officer catches up with me but he doesn't say anything, just stays close as I walk up the blood-and-flesh-spattered staircase, stepping carefully around the shards of a crystal vase.

The door to the office is open. A policewoman just outside steps forward when she sees us.

"Are you sure this is a good idea?" she asks the officer shadowing me. "It's pretty gory in there."

This makes me laugh, which is definitely inappropriate but I can't help it. "Do know what I've been through in the past thirteen hours?" I ask her when I manage to control myself. "Do you know what I've seen?"

The officer with me starts to speak but she holds up her hand. "If you're sure then go ahead," she says to me.

I do.

John is still wearing his suit, which still looks neat and pressed. His shoes are still polished to a shine and his hair is still the same salt and pepper comb-over. I look at the hands that wiped away my tears when my dad missed my tenth birthday, the hands that taught me how to tie lace-up shoes. They are the same as well. The only difference is that his body now hangs several feet over the desk, dangling from a noose he made out of electrical wire. His eyes bulge, white foam is on his lips, and his neck bends at an impossible angle.

This is the man who was a second father to me my whole life and the man who killed my dad and tried to kill me. I will probably never be able to reconcile those things, but at least I now know one thing: John Avery is gone.

I realize I am holding my breath and I let it out in a whoosh.

"Have you seen what you needed to see?" The policewoman's voice is kind.

"Yeah," I say. I'm ready to leave this room and John behind.

She walks out with me. "You said he is the one behind the hostage situation?"

"Yes," I answer as we head back down the stairs.

"I hope we can find the proof of it," she says. "So far it seems he's done a good job at covering his tracks, but of course we've barely started the investigation."

I clear my throat. "I have something that might help," I say hoarsely. "Just give me a second and I'll get it."

I'm not sure it will mean very much but maybe it's a starting point for them, a reason to make John the top suspect. Which shouldn't matter much since he's dead but it does matter, at least to me.

I walk out the front door, into the bright fall day, the clean smell of falling leaves and mowed grass almost covering up the other smells that have soaked into the lawn. But they will always be there, even when they are hidden deep in the earth.

I head over to the body bags and go to the second-to-last one on the left side. I kneel down and close my eyes for a second, trying to draw breath into my wooden lungs. Then I unzip the bag.

Nico's skin is a sickly yellow and his cheeks are sunken, making his face slightly distorted. I rest my hand on his stiff hair for a moment but even that feels wrong, sticky, probably from the blood that soaks his chest and shoulders. I slide my hand into his jacket pocket, my fingers fighting the heavy, wet fabric. I pull out the phone, which has a thin sheen of blood on it but lights up when I press it, before quickly shutting back down. The link between John and the security is right here, just a recharged battery away.

"Thank you," I whisper to Nico. It's not just for keeping the phone safe or even just for saving my life, but he will know that. Just like he knew me.

This night has gouged out my insides, leaving a ragged wound so deep it will never heal. I know I need to zip up the bag but I can't. All I want to do is crawl in next to him, close my eyes, and go with him, leaving the ravages of my life, the loss of my dad and my friends, the suffocating guilt, behind. I am ruined by this wound, there's nothing to keep me here, not now. My body gives out under me, my face now on the driveway. I can't imagine ever moving from this spot.

I am distantly aware of a car pulling up but it doesn't really register until the door slams and someone is calling my name in joy. Abby.

I pull myself up to hands and knees and look down at Nico. My sister's voice is light in my ears and I know that I am looking at a choice that is bigger than just standing up or staying curled in a ball on the driveway.

I look at his face one last time and I know what he would choose and what he would want me to choose. So I reach deep for every last bit of strength I have and I stand up.

Abby is running toward me and I meet her halfway, grabbing her up and holding her close, drinking in the feel of her sweet little face against mine, her fingers curling in my hair, her sigh of delight as I kiss her temple.

I am still broken by what happened here, by what I lost, and I know that part of me will never heal. But I have Sera and my dad's company and Abby, I have Abby.

It is enough to keep me here.

CHAPTER 35

Sera

One week later, the halls of NCCD are crowded. The last bell just rang and most of us are packing up to go home, just the jocks and debaters are heading for practice. It's like any other Friday afternoon, people running down the polished wooden floors, grabbing stuff out of their oversized lockers, looking at the screens hung up on the walls that flash information about next week's big game against Greenwich, SAT prep classes on Mondays, and the half-day next Thursday.

"Bye Sera," Cassidy calls, giving a little wave as she passes me in the hall on the way to cheerleading practice. Her finger is still in a splint but other than that she is the same golden-headed cheerleader as always.

I slam my locker shut and hoist my bag over my good shoulder. Carson walks by with a few other football players and he reaches out to give me a silent high-five, which is what all the football guys do, as though actual words are beneath them.

It is though everything is the same as it was before Mexico, before my months as a pariah, before the party.

But you don't have to look too closely to see that really it's all different now. There are piles of flowers by Mike, Lulu, and Ella's lockers, marking an emptiness that will always be there. People stuff money into the boxes that are collecting funds to bring cupcakes and balloons to Ravi, to send care packages of French chocolate to Franz.

The biggest differences are the ones you can't see though. I'm not sure how they've changed Cassidy and Carson and everyone else who was there that night. It'll probably be a long time before I fully understand how they have changed me. But there are certain things I know now, certain things I do now because they matter.

I call my sister and tell her I love her, even though she laughs and calls me a cornball. I hug my mom when I come home from school and I let my dad cook me eggs in the morning because it makes him happy. I sit with Ariel in what used to be a guest bedroom but is now her room, chatting about things like movies and TV, or just sitting, silent, being with her so she knows that she is not alone.

I also work really hard in my classes. Ariel has a clear career path now and I want that too. I'm not sure exactly what I want to do but I want it to be meaningful, for my life to be about more than just me. So while I know I'm a shoo-in for Brown, I want to earn it as well, to arrive knowing it was my work that got me there, not the silver spoon in my mouth.

There are also other changes, the dark ones, the ones that wake me up in the middle of the night in a cold sweat, reliving the stabbing of The Assassin or Mike's death. Those are the changes that have me scanning a room before I walk into it and always needing to sit facing the door in a restaurant, that get my heart pounding when I see someone in army green. I'm not sure if these will fade over time but I suspect I will always carry a shadow of them.

A couple of freshman are walking by and I tune into their conversation when I realize they are talking about last night's Letterman.

"I don't know, I think he's kind of a jerk for lying about his family," the first girl says, fluffing her blond curls.

"But at least he admitted it," her friend says. "And he looked awfully good doing it."

"Did you see his oldest brother when Letterman had his whole family come out on stage?" the third girl asks. She is rifling through her bag and pulls out a tube of lip gloss. "He is way hotter than Hudson."

Not true, I think silently as their voices fade down the hall.

As soon as he got plugged back into the world Hudson wasted no time coming clean about his family and how he lied. It's been the talk of every gossip site out there, with some people skewering him and others calling him a hero for stepping forward. He's been on an intense media tour and while he was in LA he did a big fund-raising concert for tornado victims in the Midwest. He's looking for something more meaningful too, though I wouldn't know what he's thinking about it. He warned me he'd probably be too busy to call but at the time I didn't realize how crummy that was going to feel. A week later it's like I never even knew him, like that kiss is a figment of my imagination.

I can't say I'm happy about it but I figure it is what it is. Maybe our connection was just meant to be for those fifteen hours. Maybe we both have too much else we need to be focusing on right now. Plus, when do romances between rock stars and flat-chested high school girls actually work out? I don't need the drama of a long-distance romance with a guy who has models throwing themselves at him every night.

I just wish I didn't miss him so much.

I slam my locker, sling my pink book bag over my shoulder, and head for the front door. Abby will be over in a little while and if Ariel feels up to it we will go to the playground and maybe even get ice cream afterwards. Otherwise we will just stay in and help Abby create an elaborate tea party for the stuffed animal collection that is starting to pile up in Ariel's room.

A sophomore guy holds the door open for me and I walk out into the bright afternoon sunlight, blinking as my eyes adjust. And then I stop.

A sleek black car waits at the curb, quite possibly a Porsche 911 though my heart is pounding so much it's hard to focus on details like that. Because slouching against the car in beat-up jeans and a black T-shirt, his eyes hidden by sunglasses and his hands holding the biggest bouquet of lilacs I've ever seen, is Hudson.

When he sees me he smiles a slow smile that sends shivers down my whole body. And then my bag is flying off my shoulder and I am running, squealing, jumping into his arms.

Let the drama begin.

CHAPTER 36

Ariel

It is the last time I will be here, in the house where I grew up, and I take my time, going from room to room to make sure I have all that I want. The floors have been scoured clean, the walls washed, and soon it will go on the market looking pristine and luxurious, all signs of the horror that took place here scrubbed away. The mist will always be here though, clinging to the walls and drifting through the hallways.

I don't take a lot. Clothes, shoes, books, the stuffed frog my mom got me when we went to Disneyland when I was seven. The photo album, of course, and the pictures of my parents.

My last stop is the small room on top of the garage, the room where Nico lived. It smells like him, a mix of fresh soil and Ivory soap, and this brings tears to my eyes. I'm not sure what might have been. Relationships between penniless gardeners and rich girls work best in the movies. In reality money makes things really complicated, one of the many things I learned when my dad's right-hand man killed him over it. But I know that Nico and I had a connection, that it meant something. Maybe we weren't going to be a great love affair, though that kiss was pretty amazing, but I do know we would have been lifelong friends. And I really would have liked that.

The room is sparse, a vase of fall flowers cut from the garden that have now wilted, a few pictures of his family, a pile of books in Spanish. I take the pictures and the most well-worn book, as well as the red T-shirt lying on the bed. There's more there but I don't need it and I want his family back in El Salvador to have it. Back when the bag holding his body was finally loaded for the trip to the morgue, I thought he was leaving me. And of course in the obvious way he was, or already had. But I didn't realize that next to the emptiness, the absence I will always feel, there would come to rest a little piece of him, the piece that belongs to me. So in some way he will never leave me.

I walk down the stairs and out into the yard. Landscapers have been hard at work and the front lawn is satin smooth and emerald green, like the tire tracks and blood stains were never there.

I head for my car and start loading my stuff into the trunk. The pictures, the frog, and Nico's things go on the front seat next to me. Then I get in, turn the key in the ignition, and drive down the driveway one final time. I don't look back because what matters now are the things that come next. Staying at Sera's, seeing Abby, and then in the fall, Harvard. I will choose Harvard because of the business program and I will get my MBA from them too, so that I will be near Abby as she grows up. That is also why I will establish my branch of Barett Pharmaceuticals in Boston.

The lawyers say the copy of my dad's will will hold up and I will be named the heir. Next month, as long as I feel strong enough, I will go into the city and meet with the board, to select the person who will run the main company, for now, while I am learning, but probably beyond that as well. I'm not so interested in the money-making part, I'm more interested in what we do with that money.

I am driving along the wooded road, the tall trees majestic with red, orange, and yellow leaves, sunlight slipping through to make lacy patterns on the road.

I will start up carefully, gathering a team of researchers to see what agencies that help refugees truly help them, and then giving them money so that they can do more. Maybe one of them will find a kid who loves flowers so that one day he grows up to run his own gardening shop and be in charge of his own destiny instead of a pawn to people with power. Later it will grow into the agency I will found that provides funds for homes, food, and schooling.

I am now at the edge of the trees and the space above me opens so that sun streams down, the sky wide and open and stretching before me as I drive.

What I learn from my agency here will inform the next project, the one I start in El Salvador.

The one I will name Victory of the People.